THE FINAL BETRAYAL

DI SALLY PARKER
BOOK 16

M A COMLEY

Copyright © 2025 by M A Comley

All rights reserved.

No part of this book may be reproduced in any form or by any electronic or mechanical means, including information storage and retrieval systems, without written permission from the author, except for the use of brief quotations in a book review.

❋ Created with Vellum

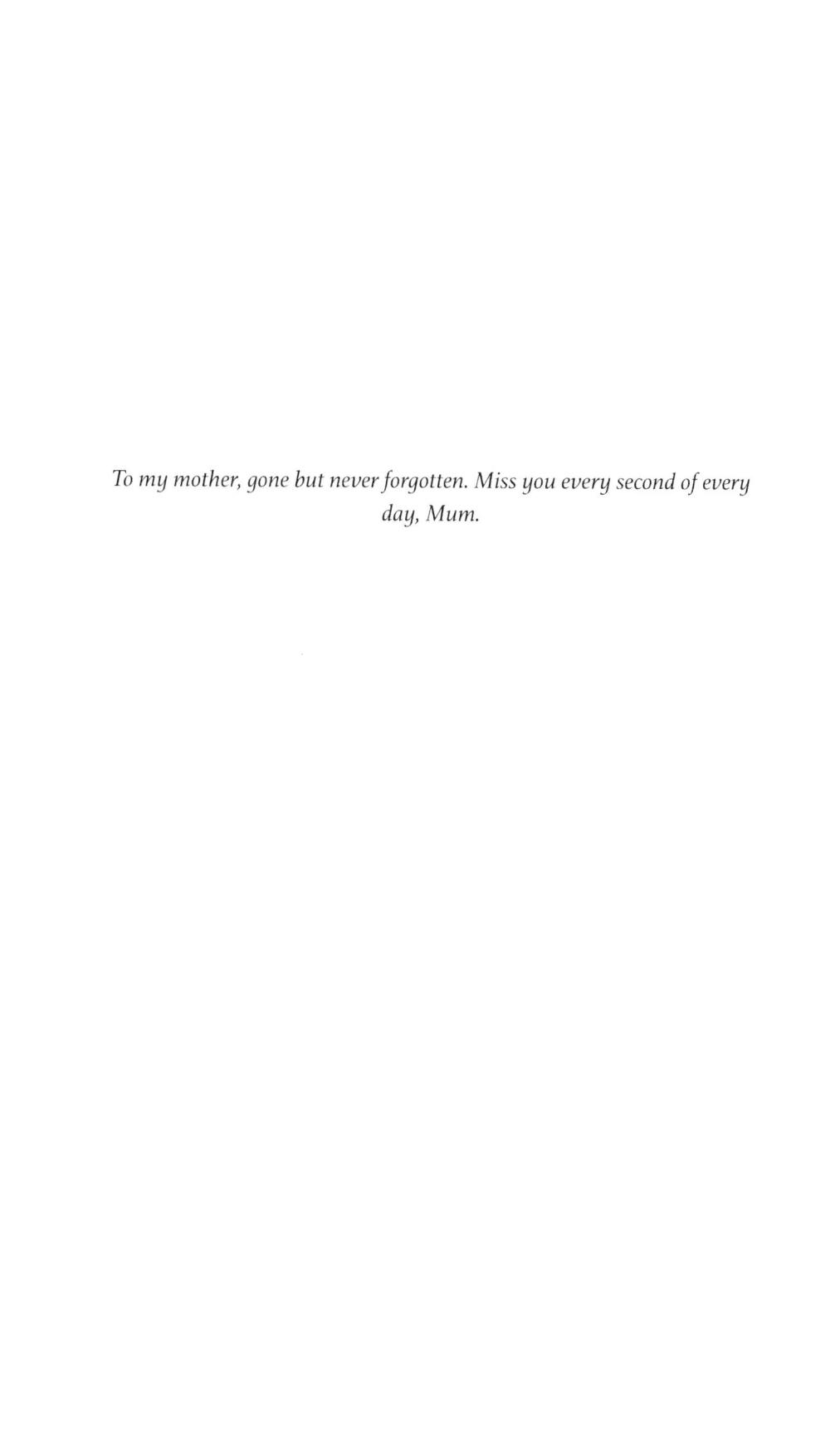

To my mother, gone but never forgotten. Miss you every second of every day, Mum.

ACKNOWLEDGMENTS

Special thanks as always go to @studioenp for their superb cover design expertise.

My heartfelt thanks go to my wonderful editor Emmy, my proofreaders Joseph and Barbara for spotting all the lingering nits.

A special shoutout to all my wonderful ARC Group, who help to keep me sane.

PROLOGUE

She strolled along the narrow path at the edge of the canal. The daylight was fading quickly now, and she was already regretting her decision to take the shortcut home. Why? She couldn't put her finger on that, but there it was, an unnerving feeling in her gut that she couldn't shift. Every strange sound sent a shiver up her spine.

A bubble emerged in the canal beside her.

What the fuck is that all about? Davina upped her pace. *Why did I wear these heels, knowing that my car would be out of action today? I'm such a bloody idiot.*

The tunnel loomed ahead of her, and her heart rate escalated. Why, why, why had she chosen to take this route? The girls in the office had warned her not to. One or two of them had even volunteered to go out of their way and offer her a lift, but she was a strong, independent woman—unflappable, usually. So why was she on the verge of crapping herself?

From the bushes to her left, she heard a scraping sound that forced her to walk faster. The light dimmed the closer she got to the tunnel, as the building blocked out the rays from the streetlights. She peered through the darkness. Was that a shadow ahead of her? She glanced over her shoulder, caught in a quandary about whether to turn back. By this time, she was at least ten minutes into her journey, and she could already feel the blisters swelling on the balls of her feet. Again, she cursed herself for choosing the wrong footwear.

She scoured the area ahead of her and put the shadow down to her imagination playing tricks on her. So, she bit the bullet and ploughed on ahead. As she got closer to the tunnel, she went up on her tiptoes and swallowed down the bile burning the back of her throat.

Two feet in, she began to relax and walked properly through the rest of the enclosed area. That was until a figure jumped out in front of her. She screamed, but the man silenced her with a slap.

"Scream again and I'll kill you."

"I won't... I promise. Please don't hurt me."

"Shut up. Now, this is what we're going to do: you're going to walk arm in arm with me. If anyone approaches us, you're going to smile and pretend that we're lovers out on a leisurely stroll together. If you show any sign of distress or plea for help, your sister will be killed. I have a man outside her house now, waiting for my call. Have I made myself clear?"

"Oh my God, not my sister. Do what you like to me, but please, please leave my kid sister out of this."

"That's down to you."

"I'll do what you want."

"Good, I knew you would see sense. Now, let's go, shall we?"

He hooked his arm through hers, and they set off. Davina shook, her fear mounting with every step they took. After they had walked fifty feet or so, a man and a woman joined the path up ahead and walked towards them.

He looked her way and whispered in her ear, "One false move and your sister will be killed."

"I understand." Playing along, Davina laughed and leaned her head on his shoulder.

"That's my girl. Good enough to get you an Oscar, I'd say."

He let out a sinister laugh that chilled Davina to the bone.

Please, please, don't let this man hurt me or my sister. What does he want from me? I have nothing to offer him. What the hell is going to happen to me? Should I risk it and scream? No, I can't do that.

He leaned in and whispered, "What's going through that mind of yours?"

"Nothing. I'm scared. No, I'm terrified. I don't know what you want from me."

"All will become clear soon enough, my dear Davina."

"Do I know you?"

He laughed again. "All will be revealed soon. Now, hush. Let's enjoy our stroll. What a delightful evening it is, don't you agree?"

"Yes."

"Have you had a productive day at work? Sold many houses, have you, today? I hear the market in London is booming at the moment, isn't it?"

Her heart pounded, and her breathing became laboured. "That's correct. I've sold three properties today."

"Nice. What percentage commission will you get from your efforts?"

"Not much. I will receive between five hundred and a thousand pounds, but only if the sale goes through."

"You're in the wrong business. We'll have a chat later. I can sort you out with a better deal than that, if you're up for it."

"I don't think so. I enjoy working where I am. I have a promotion coming my way soon."

He gripped the back of her neck and forced her to look at him. "It wasn't an offer as such. You, my dear Davina, are going to earn me a lot of money."

"What? How? By selling properties?"

He ignored her and tucked her arm through his and steered her up the slight incline and on to the main road. He dug into his pocket and removed his car keys. The lights on a nearby SUV flashed, and the doors clunked. He opened the passenger door. "Get in."

"Where are you taking me?"

"You'll see."

A couple walked past. He kissed her, silencing her in case she screamed. His lips felt strange, as if they were made of rubber. He pulled back, and she wiped a hand over her mouth.

"Enjoy that, did you?"

She stared at him, unsure if he wanted to hear the truth or not.

He shoved her in the car and secured her seat belt in place. "Move and... well, you know what will happen."

Davina nodded. He slammed the door. She watched him casually walk around the front of the car, acting as though he didn't have a care in the world. Her insides churned, making her feel queasy, while her mind kept conjuring up all sorts of vile ideas about what he was going to do to her. She glanced at the handle on the door, tempted to escape, but his warning about going after her sister rebounded in her head. She was trapped. There was no other word for it.

He jumped into the driver's seat and smiled at her. The light from a nearby streetlight showed his face properly. She was right. She *had* felt rubber when he'd kissed her. He was wearing a mask. One that was lifelike and resembled a well-known pop star, whose name was on the tip of her tongue.

He laughed again, amused by the confusion written on her face. "Thought you'd recognise me in the light, did you?"

"Who are you? What do you want from me?"

He ignored her questions, started the engine, and when a gap appeared in the traffic, he put his foot down and sped away. Not long after, he pulled into another parking space and removed something from the glove box. A blindfold. He flung it at her and ordered, "Put it on."

She covered her eyes, which, in turn, made her feel even more vulnerable—if that were possible. Tears emerged, and she silently cried, sensing that she was in a heap of trouble and there was no way out of her predicament. He'd already shown how violent he could be, and there was also his threat to kill her sister lingering in her mind. It was enough to keep any thoughts of retaliation at bay, for now.

She tried to get a sense of which direction they were going in, but it was useless. Around ten minutes later, she heard the crunching of gravel before the car came to a halt.

"We're here."

She attempted to remove the blindfold.

He slapped her hands away. "Leave it on. I'll come round and get you. I'll then guide you inside to a secret room I have created for you."

"For me? Have you intentionally kidnapped me?"

"Doh! Dumb question number two thousand and ten. Of course I have. Don't forget, I have a man outside your sister's house as backup."

"Sorry, yes, I'm stupid. Please, won't you tell me what this is all about? If you let me go, I promise I won't go to the police or tell anyone what you've done to me."

He leaned in, and she felt his breath close to her cheek.

"You won't get the chance to tell anyone because I'm never going to let you go."

"Please, don't say that. What have I ever done to you to make you want to come after me like this? I'll try to put it right, if you'll allow me to."

He wrenched her by the arm and led her across the uneven gravel. "Shut up. I've heard enough of your whining voice for one day. Watch your step. There are three of them."

She stumbled up the first step. His grip tightened on her arm, preventing her from falling.

Davina strained an ear to listen to her surroundings. He opened the door with a key, and they walked across what sounded like a tiled hallway that seemed to stretch on endlessly. They stopped, and he appeared to be searching for something in his pockets, cursing under his breath until he found what turned out to be yet another key. He unlocked a second door and then he led her down several steps. She lost count of how many there were because the chill in the air startled her. She didn't have to be a genius to realise that he was leading her into the depths of a cellar. The dust and oily smell seeped into her nostrils.

"Don't leave me down here, please."

"Stop whining. It's not going to do you any good."

Another door creaked open. He removed the blindfold. She blinked, forcing her eyes to adjust to the dim light. She was right; they were in a cellar, and now he was about to put her in some kind of cage.

Her chin quivered, and tears welled up. "Please, I'm begging you. Don't do this to me. I'll do anything you want me to do."

"Oh, believe me, I know you will. But first, you need to suffer. Now, remove your clothes."

She vigorously shook her head at the bizarre request. "No, I don't want to."

He took a step towards her and ripped the lapel off her expensive jacket, which had recently cost her a month's salary.

"Please, no more. I'll do it. But… I'm going to freeze down here."

The mask wrinkled into a kind of grin. "Maybe that's the aim."

He left her to strip down to her undies and collected something from behind her. He handed it to her. It was a sack with holes for arms and legs slotted into the material. "Put that on."

"What? I can't wear that. It'll be too rough against my skin."

He shrugged and turned away, scooping to collect her clothes en route. He locked the door and then removed his mask.

"You? What the fuck? You can't leave me here like this. What have I ever done to you?"

He placed a finger on his chin. "Let me think about that for a second or two. Ah, yes, the answer is 'plenty'. Make yourself comfortable. I'm going to keep you here for a while. Try to scream at any time, and I will carry out my threat: I will pick up your sister and bring her here to be with you."

Davina stared at him, dumbstruck and unsure of what to say or do next.

He let out his most sinister laugh yet, locked the door and walked back up the stairs. He switched off the light, then closed the door and bolted it.

Davina collapsed onto the metal-framed bed behind her. The mattress was wafer-thin. She placed her head in her hands and sobbed until exhaustion consumed her and she fell asleep.

1

"Will you slow down and take a breath?" Sally Parker warned her partner, Lorne Warner.

Lorne was spinning around, unsure which direction to take after the devastating news she had just received.

Carol, her psychic friend, had just helped them out on an important investigation. She stepped forward and placed her arms around Lorne. "I'm sorry, love. I didn't mean to scare you. You're going to need to calm down, or you're going to make yourself ill."

"I can't. We need to go. I need to ensure that my daughter is safe," Lorne insisted, sheer panic clear in her voice.

"I'll get you a strong cup of coffee," Sally said and crossed the room towards the drinks station.

"I don't want a coffee. I need to get on the road. Correction, *we* need to," Lorne said and faced Carol.

"I agree. Tony needs to come with us, too."

The more Carol said, the worse Lorne felt. Her daughter was in danger, and she was over a hundred miles away from them.

Why did I move here? I should have stayed in London with Charlie. She's vulnerable.

"Stop that. You're not to blame, Lorne," Carol reassured her, knowing full well what she was thinking.

"I can't help it. We need to go. Sally, can you arrange for emergency time off for me?"

"Go. Leave it to me. You're due some holiday anyway. I'll run it past the chief. I'll sort it. You and Carol should get on the road."

"What about Tony? Will Simon give him time off from the business?"

"There's only one way to find out. Do you want me to make the call?"

"Would you mind? Carol and I will go back to the house and pack a couple of bags. Tell him to hurry. Our daughter's life could be in danger." Even though Tony wasn't Charlie's real father, they had always got on well and he loved her as if she were his own.

"Just go. You're faffing around unnecessarily," Sally said. She returned to the group and hugged Lorne. "Please, stop worrying. Why don't you call her and make sure she's all right?"

Carol held up her hand to object. "I wouldn't do that. Charlie doesn't know she's in danger. It would be foolish to warn her."

"Are you serious?" Sally shouted.

"Please, I don't want you two falling out about this. I trust Carol. She wouldn't tell me that Charlie was in trouble if she didn't mean it."

"Exactly. Lorne has known me for decades. I wouldn't tell her something so important if there was nothing to it. We need to go, Lorne."

Lorne's gaze shifted between her other colleagues, then Sally and Carol. She closed her eyes, and her daughter's beautiful, terrified face entered her mind. She shook her head to rid herself of the vile image and opened her eyes again. "Let's go. Sally, if you can give Simon and Tony a call while we drive back to the house."

"Don't worry. I'll do it now. Please keep in touch. If you need me, I can be there within a couple of hours."

"What about this place? The team won't be able to run itself," Lorne replied, gobsmacked at her good friend's suggestion.

"We'll see. Call me, at least when you get there. Promise me?"

"I will. I promise. Thanks for this; I won't ever forget it."

Lorne and Carol ran down the stairs and out of the building.

The cold air smacked Lorne in the face. She paused to take an extra breath before opening the car door. "Shit, I brought Sally in to work this morning. She'll have to cadge a lift home or get Simon to pick her up."

Carol sighed heavily. "That's the least of our worries, Lorne."

"I know. It's the trivial things that occupy my mind when it's racing, imagining all sorts of ghastly terrors that lay ahead of my beautiful daughter."

"Slow down. All you need to know right now is that she's safe."

"Get in. We'll talk more on the way."

They slipped into the vehicle, and Lorne started the engine. Her leg shook, and she pressed down on the accelerator harder than she'd intended and almost reversed into a patrol car passing by. The officer blasted his horn, and she held up a hand to apologise.

"Am I risking my life travelling with you?" Carol said. Her expression was serious, but then she laughed. "I'm joking. Please be careful, it would be preferable that we make it back to your house in one piece. I think Tony should drive us to London."

"Are you forgetting he only has one leg? I tend to do most of the long-distance driving these days."

"Ah yes. Maybe that fact slipped my mind. He copes so well with his disability."

"I know. He rarely complains either. Over the last couple of years, his stump has been giving him some trouble. He's had numerous infections to deal with, which has been a grave concern for both of us."

"He'll be fine. I believe he's over the worst of it now."

"Glad to hear it. I hate seeing him suffer. He never lets it get him down. He adapted well, right from the word go. Bloody Taliban bastards, torturing him and cutting off his leg like that."

"Evil, twisted men. Tony suffered terribly at their hands, but the thing you have to remember is that he's resilient, and it was that resilience that pulled him through his horrendous ordeal."

"He's definitely one in a million. Which is why I love him so much."

"You've always made a great team, from the first time you met, even though you found him rude and obstructive."

Lorne laughed, remembering the day well. "He was definitely rude. I suppose he was a typical MI6 agent, used to working alone. We had several hurdles to overcome before I learnt to trust him."

"That came in France, didn't it?"

"It did. On the hunt for you-know-who."

"And you nailed the bastard."

"Yes. I can honestly say that I've never felt such satisfaction in taking a man's life as I had when I killed The Unicorn. Wicked thing to say, I know, but it's the truth. He put me and my family through hell. He tried to destroy us, just like he'd destroyed thousands of other families. The world is a better place without him."

"I agree. Although the experience scarred Charlie, she overcame her adversity and is now a top-class police officer, just like her mother."

"That was the biggest shock: her signing up to become a copper. She'd shown no inclination of wanting to join the Force before she was abducted. Truth be told, she was a pain in the arse, a rebel teenager."

"In the end, being abducted by that vile criminal made her a stronger person. She was one of the toughest girls amongst the group of teenagers held hostage. She helped so many of them survive their ordeal. She's always been a credit to you, Lorne. Which is why I refuse to sit back and allow anything to happen to her. I feel guilty about dragging you away like this, but at this time, it's important for all of us to be in London."

"I'm glad you told me. Can't you tell me where the danger is going to come from, though?"

"I can't. Actually, it was Pete who put out the warning."

Tears clouded Lorne's vision. "I hope he's watching over her."

"He's right beside her. He's aware that we're on our way. He'll do his best to keep her safe until we get there, sweetheart." Carol squeezed Lorne's arm.

Lorne held up her crossed fingers. "I hope so."

Two hours later, the three of them set off for London. Tony was in the front seat next to Lorne, his hand on her thigh, comforting her while she drove from Norfolk to the Big Smoke. This would only be the second time they had returned since they had up sticks to buy the dog kennel business. They had taken in many strays since then and, fortunately, found a gem of a manager to run the kennels after Sally talked Lorne into joining the Cold Case Team. Tony and Simon, Sally's husband, worked together renovating houses in the area. Their business was thriving, and Lorne felt guilty taking Tony away from his work, especially at one of the busiest times of the year.

"Thanks for coming with us," Lorne whispered. She glanced in her rearview mirror and saw that Carol was having a nap. She held a finger to her lips and pointed at the back seat.

"She must be exhausted after coming up trumps for you guys during the investigation and now having to contend with what's going on in that head of hers."

"We'd be lost without her. Saying that, I hope she's wrong about Charlie being in danger."

"That's why we're going down there, to prevent it from happening. Have you rung Charlie?"

"No. I didn't know whether to tell her that we were coming down. It's out of the ordinary. She's bound to guess that something is wrong. She's not daft."

"On your head be it. She'll be safe with us on the doorstep, Lorne. How did you wangle time off?"

"I left it to Sally to sort out, at her insistence. How did things go with Simon?"

"He was fine. Told me if we need him to let him know."

"Sally said the same. We're lucky to have them in our lives. True friends like that are few and far between these days."

"Aren't they? Although we'd be there for them if the tables were turned, so it works both ways."

"Absolutely." Lorne let out a deep sigh.

"I can tell your mind is working overtime right now."

"It is. I keep getting this vile image of Charlie and what she was forced to endure all those years ago. It's difficult to get rid of it."

"She'll be fine. I know it's hard, but try not to think about that, darling."

"It is, extremely hard. I wish Carol could tell us more about what lies ahead of us. She told me that Pete was protecting Charlie."

"That's great to know. He won't let her down."

They arrived three and a half hours later, thanks to a holdup en route due to two cars colliding at a main junction, which had caused a two-mile tailback. Carol had insisted they stay with her, and as soon as they entered the house, she set off upstairs to make up the spare bed.

"Help yourselves to coffee and something to eat. Oh my, I'll need to get some shopping in. There's barely anything in the cupboards or the fridge."

"Don't worry, we'll get a takeaway this evening and we can sort out the shopping later, once things have settled down a bit."

"That's a relief. Thank you for being so understanding. I won't be long. Make yourselves at home. I think it's tidy down there. Forgive me if it's not."

"Stop worrying," Lorne called up the stairs. "Are you sure you don't need a hand?"

"No. I'll have it sorted soon. You can make me a pot of tea, if you will. One cup is never enough for me."

"Consider it done."

They walked into the kitchen, which was immaculate, despite Carol telling them otherwise. Tony filled the kettle and switched it on, then held out his arms for her to walk into. "How are you holding up?"

"I'm better than I thought I would be. I'll probably crumble as soon as I lay eyes on Charlie, though."

"You're going to need to hold it together when we see her. Are you going to tell her why we're here?"

"I can't." Lorne glanced over her shoulder to make sure Carol wasn't around. "What if Carol is wrong about this?"

He cocked an eyebrow. "I'm hoping she has made a mistake, but your past dealings with her should tell you she's rarely wrong about things like this."

"I know." Lorne sighed and rested her head on his chest.

He smoothed a hand over her head.

"It's been a long day, but I'm eager to see Charlie." She peered up at him. "If you're up for it, I'd love to pop round and see her tonight. Maybe we can drop over and see her after we've eaten?"

"That's an excellent idea," Carol said from the doorway.

The kettle clicked off, and Tony finished making the drinks. "Or we could invite her round here to share a takeaway with us. What do you think?"

Lorne paused to consider the option for a moment or two, then said, "I think I'd rather go over there and surprise her."

"I think that would be for the best, too," Carol said.

"Decision made then." Tony laughed. "Have you got any takeaway menus stashed somewhere, Carol?"

"I've got some old ones in the drawer to your right, Tony. It's okay, I'll get them while you make the drinks. Can I just say that it's wonderful to have you two to myself for a while?"

Lorne hugged her dear friend. "It's always a pleasure spending time with you, Carol. Thanks for putting us up like this. It's appreciated."

"You're always welcome here, just like I am at your place. I hope the dogs are going to be all right?"

"They're in safe hands. Abby is going to stay in our spare room, so she's on hand twenty-four-seven for them."

"You landed on your feet there."

. . .

They ate an early meal, an Indian as it turned out, and then Tony drove to Charlie's house. When they got there, they were relieved to see her car parked in the drive. Charlie had moved into her new home a few years ago, after she'd broken up with her boyfriend, Brandon. To Lorne's knowledge, she hadn't had a boyfriend since then and seemed happy enough on her own.

Carol wanted to join them, but she looked and felt exhausted from her exploits during the previous investigation. Lorne tore out of the car with Tony not far behind her.

"Calm down."

"I'm so excited to see her." She rang the bell, and the door opened a few seconds later.

Instead of Charlie greeting them, a young man in his mid-to-late twenties was standing there, looking puzzled. "Hi, can I help?"

"Is Charlie here?" Lorne asked. Despite the fear rising within, she kept her voice calm and steady.

Tony stood beside her and reached for her hand.

"Who is it?" Charlie shouted out. She came to the door seconds later. "Mum... Tony... what the hell are you doing here?" She flung her arms around Lorne's neck, kissed her, and then did the same with Tony.

"We thought we'd surprise you." Lorne took a step back and gestured with her head towards the stranger. "And who's this?"

"Oh, this is Nathan... my boyfriend."

"Your *boyfriend*? You didn't mention you had a new fella," Lorne said, shocked by the news.

"Umm... it slipped my mind. Sorry. I can't believe you're here. You didn't mention you were coming down, did you?"

"It wouldn't have been a surprise then, would it? Can we come in?"

Charlie grabbed Lorne's arm and yanked her through the door. "Of course you can. It's so good to see you both."

Tony held out his hand for Nathan to shake. "Tony. It's good to meet you."

"Nathan. It's great to finally meet the two people Charlie never seems to stop talking about."

"Stop it," Charlie said. "Between you, you're embarrassing the hell out of me. Have you eaten? Where are you staying? I can make up the spare room. It's no trouble."

Lorne smirked. "One question at a time. We brought Carol back home. She persuaded us to come and stay with her for a few days. And yes, we had a takeaway when we arrived because we were all starving."

"Come through to the kitchen. I'm preparing a spaghetti bolognaise. You can tell me why she was visiting you in the first place. I haven't spoken to you in ages."

Lorne linked arms with Charlie and kissed her on the cheek. "It's lovely to see you, darling. It's been a while since you've been up to see us."

"I know. It's only due to work, I promise. It's been full-on lately."

Charlie went back to preparing the ingredients for her meal. Lorne removed her jacket and placed it on the back of a dining chair, then sat at the island on one of the stools.

"Do you want me to give you a hand?"

"No, I've got this. Do you want a drink? I've got some wine in the fridge."

"That would be lovely. Shall I get it?"

"Nope, you're guests in my house. Let me run around after you for a change."

Lorne peered over her shoulder at the two men, who were still chatting in the hallway. "He seems nice. How long have you been dating?"

"I knew it wouldn't take you long before you started interrogating me. About a month, give or take a few days."

"How did you meet?"

Charlie twisted her mouth from side to side. "Ah, yes. I'd forgotten for a moment there. I was out with my friend, Lucy. He was on a night out with one of his mates. We got chatting over a couple of drinks. We seemed to hit it off right away."

"Funny that you've never mentioned him, sweetheart."

"It wasn't intentional. It just slipped my mind. You know how it is, by the time you've asked how everyone is, any news you have gets pushed aside and forgotten about. Enough about me. Why did Carol come for a visit? Is she all right? I keep meaning to go round there and see her, but you know what it's like."

"Yep. The job comes first, eh? Only you have a new man to keep entertained now, as well." Lorne winked at her, and they both laughed.

"Don't go buying a hat just yet. It's early days, Mum. Don't read too much into it just because you're keen to see me married off."

Lorne slapped a hand over her chest. "Me? Would I? You look happy for the first time in years. That's enough for me. How's Katy and the rest of the team?"

"Katy's fine, and so is everyone else. Hey, you've avoided my question about Carol. What gives there?"

"She helped us out on a cold case we were working on. It drained her, so Tony and I decided to take a few days off to come and stay with her. You know how these things work."

"Poor Carol. I hope she recovers soon. Did she help you solve the case?"

"Massively. It was horrendous. I think it will be one of those cases that remain with all of us forever."

"Oh no. You'll have to tell me all about it later."

The men joined them.

Nathan stood beside Charlie and pecked her on the cheek. "Can I do anything to help?"

"You can sort the drinks out for Mum and Tony, if you wouldn't mind?"

He nodded. "It would be a pleasure. What would you like?"

Lorne studied him. His smile was warm and friendly and reached his icy blue eyes. She liked what she'd seen of him so far. No doubt she and Tony would swap notes later, on the journey back to Carol's.

"Charlie mentioned there's wine on offer. I'll have a glass please, as Tony is driving."

"In other words, nothing alcoholic for me," Tony was quick to add, and they all laughed.

"Go on, you're allowed one beer, which will keep you under the limit," Nathan said. "There's a Foster's lager on offer. It's all I tend to drink these days, apart from the odd glass of wine or two, now and again."

"Like at the weekend, at your friend's barbecue, you ended up blotto, and I had to call for a taxi to pick us up and drop you off the next day to collect your car," Charlie added jovially.

He placed a finger to his lips. "Shh... you're not supposed to tell your parents that. Whatever will they think of me?"

"We've all been there at one time or another throughout our lives, haven't we, Lorne?" Tony said. He sat on the stool next to her.

"We have indeed. Sorry to intrude on your evening like this. Kick us out when you start dishing up, Charlie. We can have a proper catch-up another day."

"Nonsense. If you don't mind watching us making a fool of ourselves, trying to eat the spaghetti, you're welcome to hang around. Aren't they, Nathan?"

"It's fine by me. I'm excited to learn more about what drives your mum anyway." He poured the glass of wine and slid it across the island towards Lorne.

She cocked her head. "What drives me? In what respect?"

Nathan returned the wine to the fridge and removed a can of lager, which he gave to Tony. "Do you want a glass or are you going to slum it like me?"

"I'll slum it."

They tapped their cans together and took a large swig each.

Lorne waited patiently for a response from Nathan. He glanced her way, and she noticed a twinkle in his eye that she struggled to decipher.

"In what respect?" she repeated.

"Well, Charlie always speaks about you with a sense of pride in her tone. She told me that you had retired from the Force a few times, and yet, you always return. I'm intrigued to know why?"

"Sorry, Mum. I wasn't gossiping about you, honest."

Lorne waved away her daughter's apology and considered her answer to Nathan's question. "I suppose being a police officer is in my blood, just like my father's before me." She fell quiet as unexpected tears blurred her vision. She took a sip from her glass and cleared her throat.

Her father had died several years ago. He'd never really been the same after her nemesis, The Unicorn, abducted him. The vile criminal had been the bane of her family's life. In the end, she had no other option than to hunt him down and kill him. Tony had been by her side during that dangerous mission, which had led to them falling in love. Strange really, considering the circumstances and that neither of them was looking for a new relationship.

Tony flung an arm around her shoulder. "It's still raw when she thinks about her father. Are you all right, love?"

Lorne leaned her head against his. "I'm fine. I suppose I'm more tired than I realised."

Tony kissed her on the cheek. "The last investigation was a killer. It sucked the life out of you."

"It was rather traumatic, far more than I expected it to be," Lorne agreed.

"What did it involve, Mum? Or are you sworn to secrecy?"

"Not at all. It was all over the local news. It concerned a grand house that used to be a school back in the fifties and a hospital before that, during World War II."

"Oh, I see. Dare I ask what Carol's role was in the investigation?"

Lorne took another sip and then let out a sigh. "It was very distressing for her. She brought Pete with her."

Charlie stopped stirring the sauce and stared at Lorne as if she'd lost her mind.

"Don't look at me like that. You know he's not far from us. Carol told me he's watching over you, too."

"Who's this?" Nathan jumped in to ask.

"Mum's former partner, Pete. A nasty criminal shot him."

Lorne smiled. "You can say his name, or is it still too raw for you, Charlie?"

Her daughter squirmed under her gaze. "I've tried to block it out over the years, Mum. I like to think I've moved on in my life and the bastard can no longer upset me."

Nathan's head swivelled between Lorne and Charlie, his brow creased in confusion. "Are you talking about this Unicorn fella?"

Charlie closed her eyes for a moment and then opened them and returned her focus to the bolognaise bubbling away in the pot. "Can we change the subject? Or rather get back to the conversation we were having before 'his name' cropped up?"

"Sorry, you're right. Let's move on. Anyway. It turned out that there were doorways to several rooms in the house that had been plastered over."

Charlie frowned. "Why?"

"To cover up the fact that those rooms were used to torture the kids."

"What the fu... You're kidding."

Lorne shook her head. "Nope, deadly serious. There was a lot more to it than that. But it amounts to the same. Those kids were treated appallingly, and some of them even died at the hands of their abusers."

"How awful. I hope you caught the bastards responsible?" Nathan asked, genuinely concerned.

Lorne hitched up a shoulder. "That side of the investigation is still ongoing."

"Which means they're too old to go to trial, right?" Charlie asked.

"Unfortunately, that's true."

"But surely, if they've committed the crimes, they should be punished for it, shouldn't they?" Nathan asked.

"We have several hurdles to jump over first before that can happen. Carol was able to reconnect the spirits of some of the children with their families. She did amazingly well, but the experience exhausted her."

"Poor thing. She's not getting any younger, is she? None of us are.

That was a stupid thing for me to say," Charlie said, her cheeks colouring up.

Lorne smiled. "I know what you mean. I was worried about asking for her advice, but I think between her and Pete, they were determined to do what was right by the kids involved in the heinous crimes."

"You should have seen this place," Tony chipped in. "It was enormous. I think Simon had his eye on it for a brief moment, although he soon came to his senses. It would take at least ten million to put it right after being empty all these years."

Charlie shuddered. "Who would want to bring it back to life, knowing its history?"

"Who's Simon?" Nathan asked Charlie.

"Sorry for keeping you out of the loop. He's Tony's boss, isn't he? Or are you a full partner in the business now?"

"I wish. No, Simon's my boss. But he relies on me as much as if I were a partner. Lorne and I just don't have the funds to put into the business."

"Ah, I see. And Charlie told me that you renovate houses. That's a stark contrast to being an MI6 agent."

Tony sniggered. "Yep, you could say that. Although we sometimes call on Lorne's expertise when we're decorating and furnishing the properties before we put them on the market."

Nathan frowned. "I take it you have an eye for interior design, Lorne."

"That's right. I started up an interior design business many years ago during one of my many breaks from the Force. It comes in handy now and again, but Tony and Simon have a great team around them, and they're calling on me less and less these days."

Tony nudged her. "Only because you're an excellent teacher. We're still going to need your advice in the future."

"It's great to see you both still happy in your work," Charlie said. "And how is the manager of the kennel doing?"

"Abby volunteered to stay at the house while we're away. She's amazing. We definitely fell on our feet when we found her."

"I don't know how you fit it all in, being a police officer and running a kennel at the same time," Nathan said, apparently in awe.

Lorne held out her hand, and Tony slipped his into it. "It wouldn't be possible if I didn't have this man beside me."

"Shucks, you say the sweetest things," Tony replied.

"God! Get a room, you two," Charlie groaned, seemingly embarrassed by their open show of affection in front of her new young man.

They all laughed.

"Nathan, can you lay the table for me? Are you sure you don't want to join us for dinner?" Charlie asked Lorne and Tony.

"No, we couldn't eat another thing," Lorne replied. "You enjoy it. Would you rather we sit in the lounge and wait for you to finish your meal?"

"Don't be silly. We can eat and talk at the same time, if you don't mind, Nathan?"

"It's fine by me. I'd love to get to know you more, both of you. I've heard so many tales about what you've got up to during your careers... it would be such a thrill to hear about your exciting adventures first-hand."

Lorne faced Tony and cringed. "I wonder what stories Charlie has been telling him. More importantly, I'm wondering if she's embellished the truth a touch."

"Would I?" Charlie said as she spooned bolognaise sauce over the spaghetti on two plates.

Nathan removed the cutlery from the drawer and laid the table. "I can't imagine Charlie embellishing the truth that much. She's not the type."

"Thank you," Charlie said. She placed a plate piled high with spaghetti and sauce in front of Nathan.

"This looks and smells delicious. It's a shame you're not able to join us, Lorne and Tony. Maybe we can arrange to go out to dinner one evening while you're here?"

"We'll take a rain check on that for now. I feel it's important for us to keep an eye on Carol over the next day or two."

"I understand. Maybe the next time you come down, we can revisit our plans?" Nathan's smile was charming and hit the spot.

Lorne was warming to the young man and could understand what Charlie saw in him, although, he was the absolute opposite of Brandon, her former boyfriend.

"Can I be cheeky and ask about how you lost your leg, Tony?" Nathan asked.

"No. I refuse to have that discussion while I'm eating a tomato-based sauce," Charlie complained.

"Hey, I agree," Tony said. "We can have a man-to-man discussion about it away from the ladies' delicate ears later."

"That would be great," Nathan said with all the enthusiasm of a child on Christmas morning.

"As you seem to know so much about us, we feel at a disadvantage," Lorne began. "Can you tell us a little about yourself?" She disarmed him with a charming smile of her own.

He glanced up and placed a finger on his chin. "Okay, where do I start?"

"Nathan is an entrepreneur," Charlie filled in for him.

Lorne swivelled on her stool to face Nathan at the table. "Oh, tell us more. What sort of business do you own?"

"I have several on the go, and the list would be too long. I'm bound to miss some, but I'll give you a brief rundown. I have two pubs, gastro pubs, here in London, a large café and two clothing stores; actually, one of them is a man's tailoring business. I also own the factory for that." He stared at the wall for a moment or two. "Ah, yes, I have a floating restaurant on the River Thames and two shoe shops in the city." He waved his hand. "There's more, but I don't want to bore you."

Lorne smiled. "That's mighty impressive, given your age. What about your parents? What do they do?"

"Dad died in an accident when I was young. Mum brought me up on her own, although my uncles have always stepped up to the plate and tried to do their best to fill Dad's shoes. He was a wealthy man, and I inherited a fair amount when I turned twenty-one."

"I'm glad to see you didn't waste the funds, like many youngsters would have done. Your mother must be very proud of your accomplishments."

His gaze dropped to his plate. "She is, in her own way. She's not the type to hand out praise willy-nilly. Actually, I'm glad I've had the chance to meet you both, especially you, Tony."

Tony tilted his head and asked, "Any specific reason?"

"I have a couple of properties in mind that I'm considering renovating. I would be thrilled to get your expert opinion on them. It's something I've been wanting to get into for a while now."

Tony shrugged. "Sure, I can cast my eye over them for you. When?"

"Wow, that would be amazing, thank you. The sooner the better, although I wouldn't want to intrude on any plans you've already made."

Tony glanced at Lorne. "You can spare me for a few hours tomorrow, can't you, wifey dearest?"

Lorne rolled her eyes. "If I must. I was hoping that our coming away would give us some quality time to spend with each other."

"Umm... sorry, I don't want to cause a domestic," Nathan said.

"You won't," Tony assured him. "You could come with us. That would be okay with you, wouldn't it, Nathan?"

"Again, that would be amazing. I could pick you up and ferry you around. There are two main ones I want to view, for now."

"We could meet you somewhere rather than put you out. It's no problem," Lorne suggested.

"I don't mind. It makes sense for us to go in one car. The traffic around London is getting worse every day, despite the congestion charges they've introduced."

"Whatever suits you," Tony said. "Can I write Carol's address on this envelope, Charlie? It looks like junk mail to me."

Lorne removed the envelope and handed it to her daughter to inspect.

"Yes, you're right. I haven't got around to getting rid of my crappy mail today."

Tony scribbled down the address and then took a sip from his can of lager. "What type of properties are we talking about here, Nathan?"

"One is a large detached house, and the other is a block of flats. To be honest with you, it's the flats I'm a bit hesitant about."

"As long as there is none of that dodgy cladding on it, it should be okay. We'll have a closer look tomorrow. What time?"

"About eleven. How's that? I have a meeting with some suppliers first thing."

"Sounds good to me. What about you, Lorne?"

"Yep. It gives me time to help Carol do some chores around the house." Lorne finished her glass of wine. "Why don't we leave you to enjoy the rest of your evening?"

"No, Mum, stay a while. I've barely spoken to you," Charlie pleaded.

Nathan sighed. "I apologise for dominating the conversation so far."

"Nonsense, you haven't," Lorne assured him. "I know what it's like to be young. You don't want us oldies hanging around, especially as we dropped by unannounced."

"It's fine by me," Nathan said.

"And me," Charlie said. "It's always lovely to see you both. I know I have neglected my duties in coming to visit you. I've been up to my neck in cases for months now."

"You don't have to apologise. Our feet haven't really touched the ground lately, either," Lorne said. "We all lead hectic lives. I'm just glad you've managed to find someone to share your downtime with."

Nathan reached for Charlie's hand and kissed the back of it. "We're very happy together, aren't we, Charlie?"

"We are. It's been a whirlwind month."

"You've swept her off her feet, that much is apparent, Nathan," Tony said and laughed. "Just like I did with Lorne."

Lorne shook her head and tutted. "Don't listen to him. I despised him when we first met."

"Yes, but I ground you down, or should that be, I won you over in the end?"

Lorne bashed his arm with her fist. "I saw the good in you while we were in France. Encountering a dangerous mission in a strange country certainly heightened the adrenaline rush."

"Oh, is that right? I've been disillusioned all these years. I've always thought my charm and looks were the reason you finally gave in."

Lorne let out a full belly laugh. "Wrong!"

Tony tickled her sides. "Charming."

"They're like kids when they're together," Charlie grumbled from behind them.

"I think it's wonderful to see," Nathan said. "Let's hope we're like that after ten years of marriage."

Charlie's fork hit the plate, and Lorne and Tony spun around on their stools to face them. Nathan removed something from his pocket and dropped to his knee beside Charlie.

"Charlene Simpkins, will you do me the honour of becoming my wife?"

Charlie's mouth gaped open. Her gaze drifted to Lorne and Tony, who were equally gobsmacked. Recovering, she said breathlessly, "Oh my! I don't know what to say. I never expected this, Nathan. We've never even discussed... our future together."

"Say yes," he prompted. "It's an ideal opportunity, with your parents being here. One that I didn't want to miss out on. I love you, Charlie."

Tears rolled down Charlie's cheeks. "Yes... I love you, too, I think."

Tony reached for Lorne's hand and whispered, "Well, he doesn't hang about, does he?"

"You could say that. I hope Charlie knows what she's doing."

"Don't you like him? I think he's kind of cool."

Lorne faced him and shrugged. "We don't know him well enough to form an opinion. We've only known him thirty minutes, if that."

Tony kissed her. "She'll be fine. Look at her. She couldn't be happier."

"We'll definitely have to go out for a meal now," Nathan said. "I know. What about tomorrow night? I could invite my mother along. She'd love to meet you all."

"What about it, Mum?" Charlie asked. "I'm dying to meet Nathan's mum. I've heard so much about her."

"What? You haven't met her yet?" Lorne questioned unnecessarily.

"That's what I said," Charlie replied, amused.

Nathan returned to his seat. "Is that a yes? The invitation is open to your friend, Carol, as well. Would she come?"

"She'd love it. I'll accept on her behalf. Umm… neither of us has brought any 'going out' clothes with us," Lorne said.

"We can go shopping in the afternoon, after we've looked at the properties with Nathan. It'll make a change for us to have a spend up on some new clothes," Tony added.

"Can we afford it?" Lorne asked, then mentally kicked herself for raising the subject in front of Nathan, who was obviously a wealthy young man.

"Nonsense. Of course we can. I've got a little tucked away that my wife doesn't know about."

Lorne raised an eyebrow. "Oh, you have, have you?"

"That's settled then," Nathan said. "If it's all right with you, I'm going to shoot off now. Mum hates receiving invites over the phone. I'll drop by and see her and then make the arrangements for dinner. I'll pick you up at eleven in the morning, if that's okay?" He waved the envelope in his hand. "I've got the address. Enjoy the rest of your evening." With that, he kissed Charlie on the lips, shook Lorne's and Tony's hands, and then left.

As soon as the front door shut, Lorne asked, "Does he always do everything at breakneck speed like that?"

She and Tony left their stools and joined Charlie at the table.

Charlie pushed her plate to the side and held her hand out in front of her to admire her engagement ring. "I suppose he does."

"Are you all right, Charlie?" Lorne asked.

"I think I'm still in shock. It came out of the blue. I had no inclination things had got that serious between us."

"Oh, I see. Can I ask why you accepted if you don't really know him that well?"

Charlie glanced up. "I don't know. Please, don't have a go at me, Mum. It just felt right to say yes. Maybe we can have a long engagement so we can get to know each other better."

"Good luck with that one. From what I've seen so far, he's got one speed, and that's full throttle."

"Behave, Lorne. Just be happy for Charlie. Nathan seems a decent chap. Hey, he'll have me to deal with if he messes her about." Tony laughed.

"Has your father met him?"

A sadness descended, and tears filled Charlie's eyes. "No. Umm... Dad and I haven't spoken for a few months."

"Sorry, love. I didn't know. Can I ask why? You don't have to tell me if you don't want to."

Charlie inhaled a large breath. "He's not the same. He's drinking more and..."

"And?" Lorne prompted.

"He's split up with his girlfriend. They had a massive argument, and he... hit her."

Lorne closed her eyes, and images of the awful arguments she and Tom used to have filled her mind. During their marriage, his anger had developed into mental abuse more than physical, although she could also remember several times when he'd lashed out at her. "Sorry, but in my experience, a leopard never changes its spots."

"I don't recall Dad ever striking you, Mum. Did he?"

Lorne opened her eyes and stared at her hands. Tony covered the top of her hands with his.

"Once or twice, but it was always when we were on our own."

"What a bastard. No woman should be treated like that. What is it with these men who do all their talking with their fists? Sick shits!" Charlie said.

"I'm over it, sweetheart. I've never had to deal with that with Tony." Lorne faced him and smiled. "For that I'll be forever grateful."

"It's not in me to do it. You're my equal; it's as simple as that. Yes, we have our arguments, like every other married couple in this world, but I would never dream of raising a hand to you. Only because I know I would come off worse," he joked.

Lorne kissed him. "You're a million times better than Tom. He needs to steer away from the drink; that's where his problems start."

Charlie nodded. "I agree. I told him to get help with his addiction. Until he does that, I really can't be bothered with him. Why should I be, when he isn't worried about himself?"

"Exactly. There are some people in this life who refuse to change for the better. I have no idea how our marriage lasted so long. Yes, I do. I stayed with him because I didn't want you to be brought up without a father in your life."

"You were wrong, Mum. You should have kicked him out before he lashed out at you."

Lorne shook her head. "I couldn't. He was a stay-at-home father. I was the main earner, sorry, the only one bringing any money into the house."

"He should have gone back to work as soon as I started school. He's always been a lazy bugger."

Lorne chuckled. "Don't be too hard on him. Back in the day, he believed he was doing the right thing. At least I knew you were safe." Lorne cringed. "Well, most of the time."

Charlie wagged her finger. "Let's not rake up that old crap again. I'm over it. I've moved on with my life. Nathan has showed me nothing but kindness since we started seeing each other. Lord knows what he sees in me."

"What? Are you kidding me? Have you looked in the mirror lately? You've turned into a beautiful young woman with a heart of gold. I'm so proud of who you have become. In fact, I couldn't be prouder."

"I second that," Tony said. "Nathan is a very lucky young man. We hope you'll be happy together, Charlie. Any problems, you come and see me, and I'll sort him out for you."

Charlie left her seat and hugged them. "I'm so pleased you're here. We don't see each other nearly enough nowadays."

"Maybe that will change when you get married and have kids."

Charlie returned to her seat. "Whoa! Hold your horses. Who said anything about having kids? I'm happy as I am. I have a flourishing career to consider. Why do people think getting married goes hand in hand with having kids?"

Lorne tilted her head and asked, "Have you discussed that with Nathan?"

"I haven't felt the need to. It should be obvious to him how much I love my job."

"It might be worth sitting him down to ensure he knows how serious you are about sticking with your career before you go any further," Lorne said.

"Yeah, I think that's a good idea." Charlie studied the large solitaire ring again and grinned. "I bet this cost a packet. If we split up, I could probably sell it and pay off my mortgage."

Lorne's mouth dropped open.

"I was joking. You know I'm not like most of the girls my age."

"I was going to remind you that I raised you to be better than that."

"There's no need, Mum. I know you did. Does anyone want a coffee, or something stronger?"

"A coffee would be lovely. You make that and I'll do the washing-up for you. Tony can wipe."

"Sure, why not? Anything to keep my adorable wife happy," he muttered.

Between them, they cleared up the kitchen in no time at all, then retired to the lounge to have their coffee.

"We'll have this, then we'd better get back to Carol," Lorne said. "This was only supposed to be a quick visit. It is lovely to catch up with you, Charlie. We've both missed you, haven't we, Tony?"

"That goes without saying."

"How are Katy, AJ and the baby doing?"

"The baby is now four years old and being a little diva, according to Katy. They seem happy enough. AJ is still managing to run his children's party business, as well as raising Georgie."

"They're busy people by the sounds of it. I hope the child doesn't suffer in the long term," Lorne said.

"I don't think so. I popped over there for dinner a couple of weekends back, and they all seemed happy enough to me."

"And how is work going?"

"What you meant to ask was, how is Sean Roberts, right?"

Lorne grinned. "You know me so well. Yes, how is the little shit?"

They all laughed.

"To be fair, he's always been as good as gold with me. Appreciated my talents."

"Oh, right. It must have been me rubbing him up the wrong way then. I had a difficult time with him throughout my career. Glad he hasn't taken his mood swings out on you."

"He hasn't, so far. Please don't tell me you intend dropping in to say hello while you're here?"

"No chance of that."

"Phew."

They chatted for another thirty minutes before Tony announced they should be getting back. They left just before nine.

Charlie hugged them both tightly and saw them to the door. "I'll let you know what Nathan's plans are tomorrow."

"Don't forget we'll be seeing him in the morning."

"Ah, yes. Well, have fun. I'm glad he asked for your opinion on the properties before going ahead with the purchases. It's always good to get an expert's opinion."

"We'll see. Sleep well," Tony replied and kissed Charlie on the cheek.

Lorne hugged her daughter and didn't want to let go.

Charlie had to push her away in the end. "You're suffocating me, woman. See you tomorrow."

In the car, Lorne fell quiet.

"Is everything okay?" Tony asked. He rested a hand on her knee.

"I think so. Actually, it's hard to describe how I'm feeling. My little girl, sorry, our little girl, is getting married. Who'd have thunk it?"

"I know. I always thought Brandon was the one she'd settle down with. He was such a nice guy, but I suppose he was too set in his ways for Charlie. I like Nathan. He seems a caring young man. It was a bit of a shock, him proposing in front of us like that."

"Wasn't it? It blew me away. I would have liked the chance to get to know him better before he popped the question."

"What do you think Tom will say when he eventually finds out?" Tony asked.

"I dread to think. That man needs a kick up the arse. He's wasted so much of his life already. He'll never change. We can't interfere in their relationship, I refuse to. I've always allowed Charlie to make her own mind up where Tom is concerned. I think she's finally seen him for the prick he really is. Saying that, he's still her father."

"Some father, eh?"

"He's got one thing going for him."

Tony faced her quickly and asked, "What's that?" His focus returned to the road ahead.

"He's not a mass murderer."

Tony laughed. "There is that. I suppose he should be given some slack, in that case."

"If you say so." She leaned her head back and closed her eyes. "It's been a tiring day after the trip down and then meeting Charlie's future husband. That does sound strange."

"You'll get used to it, eventually."

Lorne dozed off, and Tony had to wake her when they arrived at Carol's.

"Hey, sleepyhead. We're here."

She yawned and stretched her arms above her head, hitting the roof of the car. "Oops, I forgot where I was then. Sorry for zonking out on you."

"You were knackered."

They exited the car and walked up the path to the front door. Lorne used the spare key Carol had given her to let them in. She strained an ear. The house was silent. "She must be in bed. We'd better be quiet."

"Shall we go up?"

Lorne nodded, and they ascended the stairs. She stopped outside Carol's room. The light was out, but the door was ajar. She eased it open and whispered, "Are you awake?"

"Yes, yes. Come in, Lorne. Don't turn the light on, though. I've got the worst migraine ever. Come and tell me how it went with Charlie."

Carol patted the bed beside her, and Lorne sat down.

"Are you sure? You should be resting, not chatting with me. It can wait until the morning."

"No, I insist. I need to know how Charlie is. I've been worried about her since we got back, before that even."

"She's fine. Honestly, she's the happiest I've ever seen her."

"That's a relief. You didn't let on that we're worried about her safety, did you?"

"No, we didn't mention it at all. To be honest, we didn't get the chance to. Umm... we were greeted at the door by her new fella."

"Really?" Carol propped the pillow up behind her and switched on the bedside light but swiftly turned it off again. "Ouch, I wish I hadn't done that. Tell me more. What's he like? It's strange that I haven't picked up anything about him."

"He seems like a nice chap. He's called Nathan. He wanted to know all about us. I think Charlie has given him some facts, but not too many. He asked Tony about what happened to his leg."

"Blimey, really? On your first date?"

They both laughed.

"We told him that story could wait for another time."

"What does he do for a living?"

"He's an entrepreneur. Got his finger in so many pies, or so it seems. He's asked Tony to give him some advice about a couple of properties he wants to purchase. We've agreed to visit the sites in the morning, if that's okay with you."

"You don't have to be concerned about me. Your time is your own.

If that's what you want to do while you're here, don't let me stand in your way."

"There's more. He wants us all, you included, to join him for a meal along with his mother tomorrow evening."

"Why me?"

"Because we're staying with you, I guess. Not only that, Charlie has always regarded you as part of the family."

"I'll have to see what tomorrow brings. I can't see this headache buggering off anytime soon."

"We'll see how you are in the morning." Lorne leaned over and kissed her dear friend on the cheek. "I'll leave you to get some rest now." She stood and hesitated before she left the room.

"What aren't you telling me, Lorne Warner?"

"Umm... there's no fooling you, is there? While they were eating dinner, Tony and I were sat on the stools at the island."

"Get on with it. I get the picture. What happened?"

"God, even when you're ill, you're an impatient bugger."

"So, stop teasing and tell me."

Lorne stared at her and said, "Nathan dropped onto one knee..."

"No! He proposed? Oh my, and what did Charlie say in response?"

"She said yes, with tears streaming down her cheeks."

"And how long have they been seeing each other?"

"About a month!"

"Wow, how romantic. Was it?"

"Truthfully? I felt a tad uncomfortable to witness it. It was the first time we'd met him, and Charlie hasn't even met his mother yet."

"And what about his father?"

"He died in an accident when Nathan was a child. His mother was the one who raised him, along with several uncles. That's what he told us."

"That's a shame. His mother obviously did a good job if he has several businesses under his belt. Maybe you'll have a bunch of grandkids running around soon."

"I doubt it. Charlie is committed to her career. They haven't even discussed having children or getting married, come to that. Why would they, after such a brief time together?"

"Okay, I'm sensing some hesitation on your part. What's your gut telling you?"

"It hasn't given me any indication one way or the other. I'd like to spend more time with him before I decide if I like him or not."

"A word of warning: Charlie isn't daft. She's a highly intelligent young woman, so my advice would be to hold back on saying anything detrimental about him."

"Thanks, I will. Now, go to sleep. It'll be the best thing for you, Carol. Goodnight, love."

"Goodnight. Try not to let your mind work overtime when you go to bed."

Lorne chuckled. "I won't." She closed the door on the way out and joined Tony in the spare bedroom.

"How is she?"

"She's got a stinker of a migraine. Hopefully, getting a good night's sleep will get rid of it."

"Did you tell her about the proposal?"

"I did. She was as blown away about it as we were."

"What? Did she suspect it was going to happen?"

Lorne removed her jumper and jeans and collected her nightdress from the holdall. "No, she was as much in the dark about it as we were. She didn't even pick up that Charlie was seeing someone, let alone that she was about to get engaged to him."

"That's strange, isn't it?" He lowered his voice to add, "Carol has always been able to tell us the ins and outs of a duck's arse."

Lorne slipped off her underwear and pulled on her nightie. "Exactly. Now she's suffering from migraines and is tired all the time. I hope there isn't more to it."

"Maybe try to get her to see a doctor in the morning."

"I can try."

Her mobile rang, and Sally's name lit up her screen. "It's Sal."

"Take it. I'm going to the little boys' room, anyway."

"Which means you'll be gone hours."

"Giving you time to have a good old chinwag with your mate."

Lorne smiled and winked at him then jumped into bed before she answered her phone. "Hey, you beat me to it. I was about to give you a call."

"How are things? Have you managed to see Charlie yet?"

"Yes, all's good there. I haven't told her why we've come down here. How are things there?"

"Quiet. We're tying up the paperwork on the last case. That's going to keep us busy for a while. How was Charlie?"

"All good, I promise. In fact, we met her new fella tonight."

"Wow! What's he like? Did you know she was seeing someone?"

"No, it came as a complete shock to both of us. He seems like a nice chap."

"Is he a copper?"

"No. He's an entrepreneur. He's got several businesses on the go but is keen to become a property developer. He's asked us to have a look at a few properties he has his eye on. We're going to see them tomorrow."

"Amazing. He must be okay if he's going to be in the same line of business as Tony and Simon."

"You reckon? Umm… there's more."

"That sounds ominous. What's that?"

"He popped the question to Charlie, right in front of us."

"What question? Shit, don't answer that. Wow, did Charlie say yes?"

"Yep. We're going out to dinner tomorrow."

"What are his parents like? Do you know?"

"Charlie hasn't met his mother yet. Tragically, his father died in an accident when he was a small child."

"Oh, my goodness. That's bizarre, him popping the question without her meeting his mother first. Do you think that was on the cards for this evening, anyway?"

"It must have been. He stuck a large solitaire on her finger when he asked her."

"Holy crap. What will Charlie do? Give up her job?"

"I doubt it. She loves being a copper. It's something they're going to need to discuss in the future."

"She's a great copper, with promotions galore ahead of her. It would be a shame if she threw all that away."

"I don't think she'll do that. We'll have to wait and see. Anyway, we've got to go shopping for new outfits to wear for dinner tomorrow. We only packed a few jumpers and jeans each. We weren't expecting to go out to a swanky restaurant."

"It'll do you good to have a splurge. You deserve this, Lorne. Enjoy your time together. Ring me if you need me."

"I will. Love to both of you."

Lorne ended the call and then sat up in bed, staring at the door, her mind racing, reflecting on what had happened during the day.

Tony came out of the bathroom five minutes later. "I would steer clear of the bathroom for a while."

She tutted and shook her head. "Why do men do that?"

"What?" he asked and climbed into bed beside her.

"Look at you; you announced that as though it was a joyful experience, when it will be me who suffers from the stench."

He grinned and blew her a kiss. "There's another toilet along the hallway."

"I need to change the subject, and quickly. Do you want to get up early and shoot out to the shops in the morning? Or would you rather we left that until we've finished viewing the properties with Nathan?"

"Afterwards. We can treat ourselves to a lie-in for a change. Make the most of our time away."

"We'll see how Carol is in the morning before we make any plans like that. Did you mind? Nathan asking your opinion on the properties? It's like a busman's holiday for you, isn't it?"

"Not really. I'm always happy to help out. I'm intrigued more than anything."

"Intrigued?"

Tony pulled her in for a cuddle and kissed the top of her head. "What type of budget he's talking about. If he's minted, maybe he'd be interested in flinging some money our way."

She sat upright and stared at him. "Our way? I don't need his money. We know nothing about him for a start. How do we know he's legit?"

"All right, calm down. I didn't mean *us*-us. I was talking about Simon's business. He mentioned last week that he was thinking of developing larger projects that would need enormous investments."

"Hmm... I wouldn't mention that just yet. I think you should run it past Simon first."

"I wouldn't. Don't treat me like an idiot."

"Sorry, I wasn't. I'm just saying that we should be cautious for now until we understand what makes Nathan tick. We only spent a limited time with him this evening. Hard to judge what he's really like."

"Well, Charlie must think the world of him to say yes to his proposal. Unless you're doubting her judgement all of a sudden."

"I'm not. Stop putting words into my mouth. I wonder what his mother is like."

"Another intriguing aspect of what lies ahead of us tomorrow. I should think she'll be a strong character, much like you. She'd have to be to have brought him up on her own. She's obviously wealthy, unless all the money was left in a trust fund for him, so his mother couldn't get her hands on it."

"You're right. It's all very intriguing, isn't it? I need to check my bank account to see how much I have left to buy us each an outfit for tomorrow."

"There's no need. I said I'll treat us."

She kissed him. "My hero."

2

Charlie drove to work, and periodically, when the sun poked its head out from behind the clouds, it shone on her ring, casting shimmering patterns around the inside of the car and making her feel all excited and tingly inside. She'd pondered whether to leave it at home but decided it was too beautiful to leave it in her jewellery box.

Nathan had called just before she'd gone to sleep the previous evening and seemed as excited as she was about being engaged. Now, as she neared the station, she had to find a way of containing that excitement so she could get on with her day. She slipped her hand into her pocket and passed through the reception area.

"Morning, Charlie. Lovely day, on and off. Let's hope the sun comes out properly today. It has been a long winter to contend with," the desk sergeant said.

"It has indeed. I'll keep my fingers crossed." She would normally have held her hand up and given him a wave, but not today.

She was the first to arrive. It wasn't unusual. It was either she or Katy who was at their desk before the others in the morning. She removed her jacket and made herself a cup of coffee. Then she started up the computer to check if any new cases had come in overnight. One case in particular caught her eye from the previous day. She dug further, searching to see if another team had picked up the case yet. They hadn't.

"Morning, Charlie. You're early! Been in long, have you?" Katy swanned into the room.

Charlie immediately leapt out of her seat and poured her partner and senior officer a coffee. "Not long, about five minutes. How was your evening?"

"Traumatic. AJ and I had trouble getting Georgie off to sleep last night. She screamed the house down and complained that her tummy was sore."

"Oh no. How is she this morning?"

"She's still not right. AJ ended up spending the night on the floor in her room. She seemed to settle then. He's going to take her to the doctor this morning. Enough about me. How did your date go last night with the delectable Nathan?"

Unintentionally, Charlie ran a hand around her face.

"What the fuck is that? You have a mini iceberg sitting on your finger. He hasn't, has he?"

Charlie's cheeks warmed. She finished making Katy's coffee and handed it to her.

Katy grasped her hand for a closer inspection of the rock. She let out a low whistle. "Wow, that is truly stunning. I'll tell you something: that young man has excellent taste, unless it's a hand-me-down. Is it?"

"I'm not sure. We didn't really get around to discussing it."

Katy's brow crinkled. "Meaning what? He swept you off your feet and took you up to the bedroom, or what?"

Charlie laughed so hard she spilt her coffee. "Shit!" She ran over to the drinks area to get a cloth. "No. Hardly. We had company at the time."

"Oops, not how I imagined the scene. Who were you with? I thought you were staying at home last night and rustling up a spag bol, or am I wrong?"

"No, that's right, I did. Mum and Tony turned up as I was about to dish up."

"Lorne and Tony? How come? Are they staying with you? Did you know they were coming?"

"Slow down, one question at a time. No, I didn't know they were coming. It was a total shock. Apparently, our friend, Carol, had been up to Norfolk to help them with a case they were working on. Mum was worried about her and brought her home. She and Tony decided to take a few days off work to stay with her."

"Wow. And Nathan got down on his knee in front of them?"

"Yes. I hadn't even told them about him."

"What? I can't believe you hadn't told them. I bet that didn't go down well with Lorne."

"She was all right about it. I suppose there was a certain amount of shock factor involved. Not long after, Nathan decided to leave."

"And you were left with Lorne and Tony, no doubt bombarding you with hundreds of questions."

"You've got it. Actually, they're meeting up with him this morning."

"Without you? May I ask why?"

"Because Nathan wants to get into property developing, which was news to me. He wanted to ask their, or should I say, Tony's expert advice on a couple of properties that he's got his eye on."

"Wow. Yet more pies to put his fingers in." Katy chuckled.

"Yep, business number three thousand and ten. That might be a slight exaggeration on my part, but bloody hell, I would have thought he had enough businesses under his belt already to keep him busy."

"So, they're meeting up behind your back. How do you feel about that?"

Charlie shrugged. "Fine. I hope they get to know each other better. Hey, at least he's met my parents. I've yet to meet his mother, although, that's happening tonight. Nathan is treating us to a swanky meal out somewhere. Mum's in a panic because she hasn't brought anything to wear, not for a special occasion."

"I bet she is. Wow, this has all happened so fast, Charlie. Are you sure getting engaged so soon is what you want?"

She stared at the stone on her finger. "I wouldn't have accepted if I didn't think it was the right time. I love him."

"But do you know much about him? You've just told me you haven't even met his mother yet. It seems a bit rushed to me. Are you sure he didn't ask you because Lorne and Tony showed up out of the blue?"

"One-upmanship? Is that what you mean?"

"Yes and no."

"I doubt it because he already had the ring in his pocket."

"Ah, yes, silly me. Either way, congratulations. If anyone deserves a bucketload of happiness coming their way, it's you."

They shared a hug.

"Congratulations. I truly mean it. I hope Lorne and Tony can see the happiness Nathan brings you. I've seen a change in you since you started seeing him."

They parted.

Charlie tilted her head. "You have?"

"Of course. There's been a twinkle in your eyes for weeks now. He sounds like a good man, and he's wealthy, too, which is a bonus in my book." Katy winked and sipped at her coffee. "Good luck to you, Charlie. On a purely personal note, how is this going to affect your future working here?"

Charlie shook her head. "It isn't. I love my job, and I'm looking forward to climbing the ladder, just like you and Mum. I have a lot to live up to."

"How does Nathan feel about that?"

Charlie shrugged again. "We haven't really discussed it, not yet."

"Maybe that's something you should be considering, sooner rather than later."

"I'll sit him down at the weekend when we have more time. I'm sure he'll be fine about it. He's probably not used to dealing with a woman who has a fulfilling career."

"Tread carefully. You don't want to scare him off."

"I will, don't worry. Umm... talking about work, something happened yesterday that caught my eye. I've checked: another team hasn't been allocated the case yet. I wondered if it would be something you'd be interested in pursuing."

Charlie walked back to her desk and showed Katy the screen.

Katy read the incident report and said, "An estate agent reported missing by her boss, eh? What about her family?"

"Not sure. Do you want to take it on?"

"Why not? It's not like we're dealing with anything else other than paperwork right now. Print it off, will you? I'll get on with my post for now, until the others get here. You can hold the morning meeting for me. Give me a shout when you're about to get underway."

Charlie saluted her. Katy had been giving her more and more responsibility of late, which was fine by her. It showed how much Katy trusted her.

"I'll give you a shout. Thanks, Katy."

"What for? You'll be doing me a favour. I don't think I'm going to be at my best today after my daughter's antics last night. Keep popping your head in and make sure I haven't dropped off to sleep while dealing with my onerous chores."

"I will. Good luck."

TEN MINUTES LATER, once the team had all arrived and were settled with a cup of coffee, Charlie collected Katy from her office. "Are you ready?"

"I'm on my way." Katy tucked the unopened letters she hadn't got around to opening back into her in-tray and joined the rest of the team. She sat at Charlie's vacant desk while Charlie conducted the meeting.

"I've checked with the boss. She's given us the go-ahead to pick up this case. Davina Sedge was last seen leaving work on Tuesday night. Her car was in the garage for repairs. A colleague saw her leaving the premises and heading towards the canal, which is a shortcut to her home."

"Kind of foolish, with the nights being so dark," Stephen was quick to point out.

Charlie nodded. "I agree. No matter how many warnings we issue about people taking extra precautions, we still have to contend with cases like this. Let's start delving into her SM accounts, just in case this isn't a 'wrong time, wrong place' attack. Let's see what's lurking in her past. I'm assuming the boss and I will visit Davina's place of work this morning."

Katy nodded.

"Graham, can you check if there have been any other reports listed for the area? Anyone attempted an abduction over the past few months?"

"I'm on it, Charlie."

"Stephen, can you see what CCTV footage is available for the area between the estate agents and the canal? It might highlight someone following her. Karen, can you check Davina's social network accounts? Get a list of friends and family for us to interview later."

They both nodded.

Charlie called an end to the meeting, and Katy dipped back into her office to collect her jacket and car keys. "Are you ready to rumble?"

After tugging on her jacket, Charlie followed Katy back down the stairs.

"Did anyone notice your ring?" Katy asked.

"Karen. Nothing gets past her. That led the men to take an interest. They all congratulated me. No extra warnings came my way, thank God."

"Is that a dig?"

Charlie tutted. "No. All I'm saying is that I know this has happened quickly, but somehow it just feels right."

"Then does it matter what others think?"

"No. Not in the slightest." Charlie pinned her shoulders back and descended the stairs more confidently.

They jumped into Katy's car and drove twenty minutes to the estate agents where Davina worked.

Katy took the lead and showed her ID to the receptionist. "DI

Katy Foster and DS Charlie Simpkins. Can we speak with the manager or owner, please?"

"Oh my, yes. Is this about Davina going missing?"

"That's correct."

"I'll be right back." She scurried away and returned with a smartly dressed woman who was in her mid-forties.

"Hello, I'm Maria Crawford. Come through to my office."

They followed her through the row of desks occupied by three stunned work colleagues, into a hallway, at the end of which was a large office filled with bookcases and filing cabinets along one wall. There was a patio door behind the desk that led out into a small courtyard.

"Take a seat. I'm so pleased you're finally taking my plea for help seriously. It is totally unlike Davina to desert us like this. I *know* something bad has happened to her."

Katy and Charlie both sat.

Charlie withdrew her notebook and poised her pen, ready for what Maria had to tell them. "Perhaps you can tell us what sort of mood Davina was in when she left here on Tuesday?"

"Really happy. Well, apart from her car playing up, that is. Several of us offered to give her a lift home, rather than see her walk. She declined. Said she could do with some fresh air as it had been a long, stressful day."

"Stressful? More than normal?" Katy asked.

"Yes. It can be full-on stress around here most days. Davina is one of our best negotiators. She closed a couple of good deals on Tuesday but refused to go to the pub after work to celebrate with me."

"Do you know why?"

"Probably concerned about not having a car and getting home late."

"Why wouldn't she consider taking a taxi?"

Maria raised her eyebrow and picked up a pen to play with. "Because she had a problem with a taxi driver in her late teens and doesn't feel she can trust them."

"Fair enough. Can you tell us more about the incident?"

"Not really. I know the bloke was arrested and put in prison. He'd attacked several women. Thankfully, he turned out to be a pervert rather than a serial killer."

"And did the attack make her wary of men in general?"

"Yes, when she's on a night out. She always seems more at ease around here with the rest of the team. I still think she had a vulnerable side, though."

"Can you tell us what time she left the premises?"

"It was around five-forty by the time we'd shut everything off and put all the files away. We tend to lock the filing cabinets every night, just in case we're broken into. We have to consider our customers' personal details."

"I agree. We were told that she headed down by the canal, is that right?"

"Yes. I warned her not to. The daylight was fading, and I don't think there are that many streetlights in the area." Tears welled up. "I'm sorry for getting upset. As you'll appreciate, all I keep thinking about is why someone would take her, and all the vile images that keep surfacing are hard to deal with. She's not one to get aggressive with people."

"You don't think she's likely to put up a fight, is that what you're telling us?"

"Yes, that's right. Only because of her past experience. She confided in me that she froze, terrified, when the taxi driver assaulted her."

"How did she get out of that situation? Do you know?"

"A passerby heard her scream. The taxi driver grabbed her and threw her out of his taxi and sped off. That was how he got caught. The witness got the driver's plate number and made a statement."

"And Davina made a statement as well, I take it?"

"Yes, I believe so. I thought she was incredibly brave. She even stood up in court to testify against the driver."

"She was brave, especially as she was in her teens."

"She's such a lovely person. I hope she's not in any danger, but I fear the opposite is true."

"We'll get to the bottom of it. Have you tried calling her?"

"Yes, several times. Her phone is dead. I know she has to charge it every night as the battery is old. I keep telling her to treat herself to a new one, but she's adamant there's nothing wrong with it. Please, can you help find her? I know the statistics about people going missing are through the roof right now. I want to assure you that Davina had everything to live for. She's in the process of searching for a better property. She has a huge bonus coming her way at the end of the year."

"Have you contacted her family?"

"Sadly, her parents died a few years ago; both of them had different forms of cancer. I don't know how she coped with the loss, but she shocked all of us. Came to work as normal and continued to sell houses. I took her to one side to check if she was okay. She told me she'd rather concentrate on work than take time off to mourn her parents."

"It was her way of coping," Charlie said.

"Yes, that's what she told me."

"Does she have any siblings?"

"I think she has a sister, but I don't know much about her."

"What about her friends?" Katy asked.

"She doesn't have many. We all went out now and again because everyone gets on around here, but other than that, she prefers to stay home in the evenings. She often takes paperwork home with her, rather than sit around doing nothing. I own this place. I've got my eye on opening up a second agency ten miles away. I approached her last month about being the manager of the new office."

"And what was her response?"

"She jumped at the chance. I took a step back after I asked her, aware that our sales would probably go down here once she left, but that's the chance we have to take these days."

"Aren't the other employees up to filling her shoes?"

"No, not that I would tell them that."

"Can you give us Davina's address?"

Maria tapped at a few keys on her laptop and then scribbled

down the details, which she slid across the table to Katy. "It's not too far. I hope you find her soon. I'm going to be on tenterhooks until she's found."

"Our team is already delving into her social media accounts and searching the CCTV footage for the area around the canal. We'll organise a search team as well. Don't worry, we won't rest until we've found her."

"Thank you. Is there anything else you need to know?"

"I think we've covered everything for now. If I think of anything further, I'll call you."

She saw them back to the outer office.

"Do you mind if I have a word with the others before we leave, as you have no customers in at the moment?" Katy asked.

"Go for it." Maria clapped to gain everyone's attention. "Inspector Foster would like a quick word with you about Davina. Please tell her everything you know—it might make the difference in getting her back. I have to go; I'm late for a call with a customer."

"No problem. Thanks for your help." Katy faced the two women and the man, who were all staring at her. "It's important that we get an idea of what was going on in Davina's life recently. Did she mention to any of you if there was anything troubling her?"

The staff all shook their heads.

"No, nothing. Davina rarely spoke about her personal life while she was at work," one of the women said. "I know she didn't have a fella on the go. She ditched the last one over a year ago."

"Do you happen to know his name or anything about him?" Katy asked.

"I think he was a plumber," the same woman replied. "I can't remember his name, though, sorry."

"That's okay. We'll have a look through her social media accounts, see what we can pick up from them. What about her customers over the last few weeks or months? Anyone she was apprehensive about?"

The three of them shook their heads again.

"Okay, that's all. I'll leave a few of my cards on the desk here. Please call me if anything else comes to mind."

"Do your best for her. She's in a class of her own, and we miss her," the male said.

"Don't worry. We'll do what's needed to bring her back to you safely."

They left the premises and returned to the car.

"What now?" Charlie said.

"I think we should drop by her house, check she's not at home and possibly have a word with the neighbours while we're there."

"Makes sense. It's a mystery what's happened to her. We need to find this taxi driver and see if he's still inside or whether he's been released."

"Want me to ring the team? Get one of them to check while we're en route?"

"Good idea." Katy entered the postcode into the satnav and drove off.

"Hi, Karen, it's Charlie. We don't have a name for this bloke, but there should be a record of the offence. A taxi driver assaulted Davina when she was in her teens. A passerby came to her rescue. The driver was caught and went on trial for several charges. Can you do us a favour and check the details out for us? We need to know if the taxi driver is still serving time or if he's been released."

"I'm with you. Okay, I'll get on it now."

"Hold on. Can you also look up Davina's socials? She was seeing a plumber about a year ago. Find his details, too. We'll need to interview him in the near future."

"Will do. Anything else?"

"Not at this time. We're on our way to Davina's house. We'll see what the neighbours have to say, if anything." Charlie ended the call and rested her head back. "We haven't got a lot to go on, have we?"

"It depends. More than we usually have at this stage during an investigation."

Charlie glanced sideways. "If you say so."

. . .

DAVINA'S HOME was a mid-terraced house in the middle of a large estate. Katy knocked on the door and crouched to look through the letterbox, straining an ear for any movement inside. She stood upright and announced, "Nothing, from what I can tell. Let's check with the neighbours. I'll go right."

They split up.

Charlie knocked on the door to the left, and it was immediately opened by a woman in her seventies or eighties.

Charlie flashed her warrant card. "Hi, I'm DS Charlie Simpkins of the Met Police. My partner and I are making enquiries about Davina Sedge, who lives next door."

"You are? Has she done something wrong?"

"No. Umm… her boss has reported her missing. Can you tell me when you last saw her?"

"Now you're asking. I suppose it was a week ago when we were putting our bins out. I was late because I forgot what day it was. Missing, you say? That's strange. How do you know? Hold on." The woman peered past Charlie at the road behind her. "I can't see her car, but that's not surprising, she should be at work now. Sorry, I'm not making sense. I've been on medication, and it's messed with my head. What can I do for you?"

"I was wondering if you've seen anyone strange visiting Davina lately, or if anyone has been hanging around, perhaps?"

The lady paused and sighed. "No, I'm sorry. I can't say I have. What a shame she's gone missing. You hear such dreadful stories about what men do to women these days… well, it's terrible. Davina has always come across as a smart young lady, you know, intelligent. She is devoted to her job. I've not seen a lot of visitors come to the house. She's always seemed a bit of a loner to me. Pleasant enough to say hello when she saw me, but nothing more than that."

"Not to worry. If you see anyone suspicious hanging around, would you mind calling the station and letting us know?"

"Of course. It's the least I can do. I hope Davina reappears soon."

"So do we. Thank you for speaking with me."

The woman smiled and closed the door.

Charlie crossed the road and knocked on the house opposite. There was no answer, so she tried next door.

A man in his sixties opened the door and eyed her warily. "Can I help?"

Charlie explained the situation and asked if he'd seen any strangers hanging around lately.

"No, I don't think so. Sorry I can't help. Hope you find Davina soon."

"Thanks. Sorry to disturb you." Charlie crossed the road again as Katy said goodbye to the neighbour next door. "Any luck?"

"Nothing. You?"

"Nope. What shall we do now? Return to base?"

Katy seemed as defeated as Charlie felt. "We might as well. Let's hope the rest of the team has had better luck."

3

Lorne was still very concerned about Carol the following morning. She was refusing to get up or eat anything that Lorne prepared for her. "I think we should call a doctor out, Carol, this isn't right."

"I'll be fine later, I'm sure I will. I'll stay in bed for the rest of the day. I feel bad that you're having to entertain yourselves."

"You don't have to worry about us. We've got our day all planned out for us by the handsome Nathan."

"Ah, yes. Silly me, of course you have. I hope everything goes well. It's nice of him to want your valued opinion. It shows a willingness to make an effort with his future in-laws."

"I suppose so. Is there anything you need before we go?"

"I have everything I need, now stop worrying about me and enjoy your time here. You don't need an old fuddy-duddy like me getting in your way."

"Nonsense, you're not old. Behave yourself." Lorne leaned over and kissed Carol on the cheek. "Is there anything you need from the shops? Shall I call in at a pharmacy and see if they have a miracle cure for you? There might be some new tablets on the market that you haven't tried yet."

"Okay, yes, maybe that would be a good idea. Thank you, Lorne."

"At last. I hate feeling useless when you're obviously suffering."

"That's because you're a considerate lady, always have been, since the day I met you. Now go, please, my head is thumping."

"Sorry, yes, you're right. You shouldn't be talking. Enjoy your rest. I'll drop in and see how you are when we get back."

"Enjoy yourselves."

"We'll do our best." Lorne left the room and closed the door quietly behind her.

Tony was on the landing, waiting for her. She put a finger to her lips and gestured for him to go downstairs before they entered into a conversation.

Once they were in the kitchen and Lorne had closed the door, he asked, "How is she?"

"I'm really worried about her. I've nagged her, but she's still refusing to go to the doctor. She seems to think her head is going to clear soon. I asked if we could drop by a pharmacy and ask for their advice, and she finally relented. So, remind me to do that before Nathan drops us off."

"There's a pharmacy at the end of the road; he can drop us outside, and we can walk the rest of the way."

"I agree. Are you ready?" She glanced at the clock on the wall; it was ten minutes to eleven.

"Just about. Are you?"

"Yes, all set for the off. How are you feeling about today?"

"Excited. I'm eager to see what sort of properties have caught his eye and what kind of budget he's considering."

"I think I'm more apprehensive about meeting his mother this evening and going to a swanky restaurant."

"Don't be. She'll have to take us as she finds us. We'll splash out on a new outfit each this afternoon; that should go a long way towards you feeling more comfortable in the woman's presence. I'm intrigued to see what she looks like. It's a shame his father isn't around. Still, I suppose Nathan has done well for himself, despite not having his father to guide him."

"Hark at you. Look at how many single mums there are in this country, where the fathers have buggered off, and more to the point, how many millionaires there are out there."

Tony held his hands up. "Sorry, you're right. Trust me to say the wrong thing."

The doorbell rang, interrupting their conversation, which was a relief to Tony judging by his expression. "Saved by the bell. I'll get it."

Lorne followed him up the hallway but dipped into the lounge to collect her handbag while Tony let Nathan in. She joined them in the hallway.

Nathan smiled and leaned in for a kiss. Lorne pecked him on both cheeks.

"Lovely to see you both again. I hope you're ready for this adventure."

"We're looking forward to it," Lorne assured him.

"Onwards, we have business to attend to." He led the way out to the car.

Lorne secured the door behind them. She insisted on sitting in the back, allowing Tony to sit in the front, which would give him more room for his prosthetic leg.

The car was built for luxury, and Lorne felt comfortable as soon as she tucked her seat belt around herself. "This is lovely. Have you had it long?"

"A couple of months. My father always had the best cars. I suppose I'm taking after him. You can't match the luxury of a Mercedes. I know most men my age don't find them 'fashionable', but it's all about the comfort for me."

"It has that all right. Where is our first stop?" Lorne asked.

"About twenty minutes away. I thought we'd check out the detached house first, if that's okay with you?"

"We're in your hands. Whatever is best for you. We're eager to see what you have lined up for us, aren't we, Tony?"

"And some."

"Okay. Buckle up. Don't worry; I'm a safe driver, and I usually stick to the speed limits where possible."

Lorne sat back and enjoyed the ride to the first property. Nathan didn't really talk much while he was driving. She'd class him as a safe and steady driver. He pulled up outside a manor house which was set back from the road. Lorne glanced around her at the other properties and resisted the temptation to let out a whistle. It was an impressive area. If he was thinking of buying it for somewhere he and Charlie could call home after they were married, she sensed her daughter would feel uncomfortable living there.

Nathan pointed ahead of him. "It's this house. What do you think?"

"It's in a beautiful area," Lorne said, her eye drawn to how much garden there was at the front of the property—a rarity these days, especially in London.

"I can't wait to see inside," Tony admitted. He unhooked his seat belt and jumped out of the car then opened the back door to help Lorne out.

She accepted his hand and swivelled in her seat. It was quite a step down.

Nathan appeared and held out his arms. "Do you need a hand? It's not the easiest vehicle to get out of if you have short legs. No offence."

Lorne laughed. "None taken. Thank you. I think I can manage."

The two men took a step back, giving her the space she needed.

Nathan showed them through the immaculate front garden. "This is the best part. The house is a tip inside; squatters have been living here for several months. The weird thing is they cared for the garden but... well, you'll see for yourselves what state they've left it in."

He inserted the key in the lock. "My friend is an estate agent. He couldn't join us today, so he gave me the key."

"He must be a good friend to trust you, especially after dealing with squatters."

Nathan laughed. "He didn't. A friend of his got rid of the buggers."

"Didn't the police get involved?" Lorne asked out of curiosity.

"No, they refused to, although they attended when the raid

happened. It was all done above board through the court system. At least that's what Zach told me."

Nathan opened the large front door, and inside, the place was incredible despite the signs of neglect and damage caused by the squatters. The marbled hallway had a sweeping staircase as its main feature.

"Oh God, it's such a shame. This place is beautiful—or it could be—in the right hands," Lorne said. She turned around in the centre of the vast hallway, surveying every inch of it.

"I'm thrilled you seem to like it as much as I do. Please, let's press on, there is so much for you to see. Although I have to warn you, the kitchen is in an appalling state."

He led them through the hallway and revealed five reception rooms on the ground floor. The grand proportions of the rooms astounded Lorne. "They're magnificent. Look at the cornices. I know everywhere is a mess, but as a property developer, you need to be able to see beyond that."

"That's where I'm failing and why I needed your advice. I can envisage so much, but I'm struggling to get beyond the destruction those horrible people caused. Why don't I show you the kitchen? It's superb, but, again, it has been treated abysmally by the idiots who wormed their way into the building and set up home. How the councils allow that type of thing to happen is beyond me."

"How many people did they evict?" Tony asked as they walked towards the rear of the property.

"Over fifty."

"Oh, shit!" Lorne said and slapped a hand over her mouth. She dropped it and added, "Actually, if there were that many here, I'm surprised it's not in a worse state."

"I'd hold off on making that judgement, if I were you, until you've seen the rest of it."

Lorne pulled a face. "Ouch, okay. Lead on."

He pushed open the door in front of him. The kitchen was enormous, and as Nathan had warned them, it had been devastated by the squatters. It stank to high heaven of fried foods. Every surface was coated in grease. Lorne heaved.

Tony seemed okay with his surroundings and threw an arm around her shoulder. "Are you all right?"

"This is gross. It saddens me that someone can even think about treating a house of this stature like this. I'm imagining what it probably looked like before those mongrels got their hands on it. What a shame. It's nothing short of criminal, is it? I wish the police had more power when it came to preventing this sort of thing from happening. It's usually druggies who break into houses like this and set up home."

"That much will be evident when we get upstairs," Nathan told them. "I just want to make this place whole again, but my biggest concern is how much it is likely to cost."

"It won't be cheap," Tony admitted. "Why don't you show us the rest of it and then we can discuss it further?"

They passed a door on the right as they backed out of the kitchen.

"It even has a cellar. Unfortunately, Zach hasn't got a key for it, so I'm guessing the squatters hadn't gained access to it."

"I bet it's a wine cellar, matching the grandeur of the house," Lorne suggested.

"More than likely," Nathan agreed. "Okay, you're going to need to brace yourselves for what lies ahead. The bedrooms and bathrooms are in horrendous condition."

"I can imagine, given what we've witnessed already," Lorne said. "These types of people tend to spend day and night in bed, from what I've discovered over the years."

"Sounds about right." Nathan led the way up the grand staircase.

"How many bedrooms are there, Nathan?" Lorne asked. She was careful not to put her hands on the banister, fearing what germs she might pick up.

"Five large bedrooms and a boxroom that could be made into a dressing room or even a study. I'm inclined to go with the former. I see the study being downstairs, maybe incorporating it into a library. What do you think?"

"There are enough reception rooms to accommodate that idea," Tony agreed.

Nathan opened the door to the first bedroom. "You might need to cover your noses before you enter the room."

Lorne heaved a second time and placed a hand over her nose. It did nothing to prevent the smell of stale drugs from seeping through her fingers. "Oh, Lordy, this is unbelievable. I know you warned us what to expect, but even my imagination couldn't foresee what it would be like. How can people live like this? What possesses them to take over a stunning, elegant property like this and wreck it?"

"I'm guessing jealousy. Anyway, moving on, because time is getting away from us and I don't want to take up too much of your day."

"Don't worry. We're umm... I was about to say enjoying ourselves," Lorne said, "but that would be stretching the truth."

They left the room, refreshed the air in their lungs with slightly cleaner air and moved on to the next room.

Tony shook his head. "Ignoring the mess, the bones are good in this house. This is another grand room. There's no real structural damage; it's mostly all cosmetic that needs addressing."

"Yep, I have to agree with Tony. You've got to have the imagination to look beyond all the shit," Lorne said.

Nathan quickly showed them the rest of the bedrooms before he opened the door to the two bathrooms on the first floor.

"I'm not sure I want to see them," Lorne stated, already fearing the worst.

"Maybe we should leave them. They're in a shocking state."

"It would be better to strip out the kitchen and bathrooms and start from scratch. I would employ cleaners to come in from the word go and then assess what needs to be done," Tony said. "As to how much all this is likely to cost, I'd say around two hundred grand."

Nathan shrugged. He didn't seem put out by the figure at all. "I was thinking more like half a million, so that would be a walk in the park if your prediction is right."

Lorne raised an eyebrow at his blasé reaction. *Nice to have so much money under your belt!* "It depends on how much they're asking for a property of this size in this area of the city."

"What do you think?" Nathan asked.

Tony contemplated the question for a few moments, then announced, "You've got to be talking three to four million for a pad like this."

Nathan winked and pointed at him. "Bang on the money. Three and a half million."

"Well, if you did it up tastefully enough, I can see you adding another million to the price. It depends on whether you intend to flip it or hold on to it and start a property portfolio."

"What would you suggest?"

"Renting out has its drawbacks. No one treats a house the way you would, so five years down the line it might cost you another couple of hundred grand to put it all right again," Tony said.

"Hold on, even if you get wealthy tenants in?" Lorne asked.

"Yep. Judging by some conversations I've had with other developers in our neck of the woods."

"Shameful," Lorne said.

"It's life. People don't care these days," Tony replied.

"It's worth considering holding on to it, perhaps moving in once the work is completed." Nathan smiled and asked, "Do you think Charlie would like it here?"

Tony and Lorne glanced at each other.

Lorne faced Nathan and said, "Do you want an honest answer to that?"

Nathan crossed his arms and nodded. "Of course, I wouldn't have asked otherwise."

"I'm not sure. She's never been used to the finer things in life. Her father and I lived a simple life, and Tony and I do the same where we are."

"But Charlie is different. She's experienced so much pain and misery in the past. All I want to do is spoil her. This place would be my wedding gift to her."

Lorne's eyes widened, and she cleared her throat. "Oh my. In that case, feel free to ignore me. You must listen to what's going on in your heart."

"Yes, I agree with Lorne. I think this place would blow Charlie away once it is renovated. Has she seen it?"

"No. I'd rather keep this place a secret from her, if that's okay with you? Carrying her over the threshold after the wedding and seeing the look on her face will be the icing on the cake for me. Excuse the pun; it wasn't intended."

Tony reached for Lorne's hand and squeezed it. "You're a good man, Nathan."

"I try to be. It's how I was brought up. I try not to shove my wealth down people's throats. I hope I haven't done that today. I apologise if I have. My aim in this life is to show kindness when people least expect it. I think I fell in love with Charlie on our very first date. She's unlike any other girl I've ever known. She doesn't care about the money. She's down to earth, and I find that an attractive feature."

"Thank you, that means we raised her well," Lorne said.

"Undoubtedly. She's a pleasure to be around. My mother is going to love her. Right, shall we move on to the next property?"

Lorne and Tony nodded.

"I must admit, it's the polar opposite to this place but I've been told by Zach it would be a sound investment."

"We'll be the judge of that," Tony said. "While I trust some estate agents, most of them offer opinions that ultimately line their own pockets."

Nathan laughed and tapped the side of his nose. "I get you. Which is why I've asked you both to join me. I value your expert advice. What you've suggested so far about this house has solidified my opinion."

"Glad to hear it."

He led the way out of the property and locked the door behind them. A sadness descended over Lorne the second they left the house.

Tony nudged her. "Are you all right?"

"Yes. I feel strangely drawn to this place and I'm sad to leave it."

Nathan overheard the conversation and whispered, "That's great, another reason to go ahead and buy it. Let's hope Charlie gets the same feeling as you do when she finally sees it."

"Does that mean you've made up your mind to buy it?" Tony asked.

He pressed the key fob, and they got into the car.

"I think I have. Thanks to your valuable insight. If I get some plans drawn up, will you cast your eye over them for me?"

"It would be an honour. If you need any interior design ideas, Lorne can lend a hand there, too."

"Excellent. The day has started out so well. On to the next property."

Nathan drove to the second location, and they chatted like they were old friends. Lorne had a feeling that this young man would be a good influence and, furthermore, a great match for her daughter. She felt at ease with him. Which surprised her, given how long they had known him.

"Where were you brought up, Nathan?"

"In London. Over in Richmond Park area. Do you know that side of the city?"

"Sort of. We visited the actual park a few times on days out when I was a child. Mum and Dad loved to have a picnic. It was a cheap day out."

"I take it you didn't have a lot of money growing up?" Nathan glanced at her in the rearview mirror.

"Not just then. We don't have a lot now either. Although we're doing better than most couples I know."

"Must be difficult running the kennels and both having full-time jobs, as well."

"We cope, don't we, Tony?"

"That we do. Lorne and I make a great team. We both have the same values and ambitions in this life. I suppose that's what drew us together."

"Oh, Charlie tells a different story, that you were drawn together because of your hatred for that vile criminal who abducted her."

"She's right. That was the original motivation that brought us together." Tony reached behind him to hold Lorne's hand. "Things grew quickly between us after…"

"After?" Nathan enquired, again looking at her in the rearview.

"That period in our lives was over," Lorne hastily finished for her husband.

"It must have been horrendous dealing with such an evil man who blighted all your lives. I can't imagine the trauma Charlie went through."

"She's one of the bravest girls I know. It was her courage and determination that allowed her to escape the criminal's clutches."

"Thank goodness. Hard to believe someone like that remained at large all those years."

"That's the underground for you. Once these criminals stick together, there's no telling what they're likely to get away with."

"Thankfully, those days are behind us now, and I think we've all come through it mostly unscathed, especially Charlie," Tony said. He turned in his seat and smiled at Lorne.

She returned the smile and sighed. "Ain't that the truth? Are we nearly there?"

"Not far now. Another five to ten minutes. We've been lucky with the traffic. I hope you're both excited about this evening. I'm sure you're going to love my mother."

"I'm surprised Charlie hasn't met her yet. Is there any reason she hasn't?"

"Mum has been on an around-the-world trip. She loves cruising. I tried it once; I was sick as a dog and jumped ship the minute the boat docked. She was mortified when I told her I was flying home. Rocking about on the high seas isn't for me. Have you tried it?"

"No, we've never had the opportunity, or the funds, to go on holidays abroad, have we, Tony?"

"I'm not sure I'd want to travel these days. I've done my share over the years during my career."

"Ah, yes. Being a spy." Nathan laughed. "What's it like being a real-life James Bond?"

Tony chuckled. "It had its moments."

"Are you going to tell me about your leg? Or is that a subject you'd rather not discuss?"

Tony shrugged. "I don't mind telling you. I was captured by the Taliban. They tortured me and, well, I don't need to fill in the rest for you, do I?"

"Oh no, how terrible. How did you escape?"

"It's all a bit of a blur, really. My colleagues found me. I was bleeding to death. I was flown home and treated by good old NHS doctors."

"I always go private myself, but I'm glad we still have the NHS to fall back on these days. It was touch and go when Johnson was PM. There were a lot of rumours circulating that he wanted to sell it off."

"Not sure if that would have ever happened," Lorne said. "Saying that, Bo Jo was a law unto himself." She shuddered. "I have trouble taking that man seriously most of the time."

"He's not the best Prime Minister this country has ever had, that's for sure," Nathan agreed. "We're nearly there now. I know the area isn't a patch on where the detached house is, but it's supposed to be an up-and-coming area that has been earmarked for a regeneration budget from the council."

"That's always an excellent sign. Along with how many coffee shops are due to open." Lorne laughed.

"Ah, yes. So I believe. Here we are now."

Lorne stared at the dilapidated small block of flats. "Holy...!"

"I did warn you." Nathan parked close to the flats. "Are you sure you want to press ahead with the visit?"

"We're here now, so we might as well," Tony said.

Lorne was helped out of the car once more by her caring husband, and they approached the stairs up to the first floor.

"The rooms below are storage areas. I was thinking of turning them into garages. What do you think?"

"I would. I should imagine parking is at a premium in this part of the city," Lorne said. There was litter all over the stairwell, and the smell of urine made her cover her nose and mouth. "Not the best welcome in the world."

"Sorry, I'm already regretting bringing you here. Would you rather we give this a miss?"

Lorne shook her head. "Don't be silly. As Tony said, we're here now; we might as well see what's on offer. I doubt if my opinion is going to be swayed, though."

He unlocked the door to the first flat. It was a hellhole.

Lorne popped her head inside, but the smell hit her so badly it almost knocked her off her feet. "I can't. I'm sorry. You two go ahead without me."

"I don't think this will take long," Tony assured her.

Nathan led the way. Lorne watched them move from room to room from the safety of the concrete landing outside the flat. Tony and Nathan emerged, shaking their heads, around two minutes later.

"I think we've seen enough to realise this property isn't for me," Nathan said. "Sorry for wasting your time, folks."

Lorne waved away his concerns. "You haven't. These things have to be checked out."

"Lorne is right. You would have been wondering if this was a missed opportunity if you hadn't come here and checked it out for yourself. I think you're better off putting all your efforts into the detached house. I don't think you can go wrong there. It has extraordinary bones and will turn out to be a wonderful project if you're prepared to sink the right amount of budget into it."

Nathan locked up, and they walked back to the car.

"I agree. I'll drop you off and then pay Zach a visit to get the ball rolling. I can't thank you enough for giving up your time today."

"It's been our pleasure," Lorne said. She linked arms with Tony, and they weaved their way back through the mess in the stairwell once more. "I don't suppose you'd drop us off at the pharmacy at the top of Carol's road, would you? I need to pick up some medication for her."

"Of course."

Fifteen minutes later, he dropped them off and heaped another bout of thanks on them. "I'll see you later. I'm looking forward to chatting with you more over dinner tonight."

"And we can't wait to meet your mother and get to know you both a bit more," Lorne replied.

He sped off. Lorne and Tony entered the pharmacy.

"Do we need any toiletries?" Tony asked. "I might treat myself to some new aftershave."

"Can we afford it? Not on top of the outfits we need to buy this afternoon?" She peered over her shoulder and added, "Why don't you see if they've got any sample bottles and pick up a few of them instead? It'll be cheaper."

"Christ, what are you like? We're not that hard up, despite what you think."

"Huh! Says you. I'll be right back." She left him to it and approached the young woman at the counter. "Hi. My friend has been suffering from a bad migraine for a few days. She doesn't want to bother the doctor. I said I'd come and see if there was anything you can suggest she could take. Perhaps there's something new to the market. Is there?"

"I can ask the pharmacist to see if he can suggest anything. Is she prone to having migraines? Or is this a one-off?"

"I believe it's the first one she's had in a while."

"I'll be right back."

The assistant trotted up a couple of steps behind her. A man wearing spectacles peered over the counter at Lorne and nodded. He dipped out of view, and the assistant returned and placed a packet of pills on the counter.

"He reckons these are the best but also suggested that if the symptoms persist, your friend will need to either visit the doctor or call one out. She might not respond to tablets if it's that bad. My friend is the same. Her doctor has to give her a super-strong painkiller in the form of an injection."

Lorne cringed. "Let's hope it doesn't come to that. I'll take these for now. Thanks for the advice." She paid and then went in search of Tony. "Bloody hell, you stink."

"Charming. What do you think of this one? I think it's my favourite." He pointed to the right side of his neck.

She sniffed it and waved her hand from side to side. "It's passable." Then she sprayed a few of the others in the air and whiffed them. "I'd say this one is more suited to you."

"You mean you prefer the smell of it over the others."

"That's what I said. Come on, hurry up and decide. I'm eager to get these tablets back to Carol. I hate the thought of her suffering too long."

"This one it is then." He took the sample up to the counter to check with the assistant if it was okay to snag a bottle free of charge.

"Feel free. That's what they're there for. That one's a good choice. I bought it for my partner last Christmas. He adores it."

"Cool. Thanks very much."

On the way back to the house, they linked arms and discussed how their day had panned out so far. As soon as Carol's home came into view, Lorne knew there was something wrong. She gasped. "Oh shit!" When she saw the front door open, she unhooked her arm and ran ahead.

A neighbour was walking up the path.

"Hi, what's going on?" Lorne asked.

"I saw the door was open. I rang Carol to let her know. She screamed for help. I was on my way to assist her."

"Shit! It's okay, we're here now. My husband and I are staying with her. I'm a police officer. I might need to speak to you after I've checked how Carol is. Which side do you live?"

"The house on the right. I hope she's okay. Poor Carol. Why was the front door open? Did you leave it open?"

"I don't think so. Gosh, now I'm questioning myself. Thanks for your help."

"I'm Helen by the way."

"Lorne, and this is my husband, Tony." Lorne ventured into the house and called out for Carol. "Carol, are you all right?"

"I'm up here," a faint voice replied.

Lorne bolted up the stairs two at a time and barged into Carol's bedroom. She found her friend sitting on the edge of the bed, nursing a bloody head. "What the fuck? Did you have a fall?"

"No. Someone broke in and attacked me. If my head wasn't hurting before, it sure bloody is now. I'm in agony, Lorne. I think I need to go to the hospital. Will you take me?"

"What's going on?" Tony asked from the doorway.

"It's Carol; she's been attacked. Help me get her to the car. We need to get her an appointment with a doctor."

"Christ. Of course. Did you see who it was, Carol? Did they tell you what they wanted?"

"They took some of my jewellery. I'm not bothered about that. I'm more concerned about how the person got in. Did you close the front door on your way out?"

"I feel so guilty. I'm sure we did, but now you've got me doubting myself. We can address that later. Let's get you to the hospital and have them check you over."

They stood on either side of Carol and eased her to her feet.

As expected, she was unsteady and tottered slightly. "My head is throbbing. Oh God, I don't think I'm going to be able to move far under my own steam." With that, she passed out.

Tony immediately swept her up in his arms. "You're going to have to go ahead of me and guide me down the stairs. I won't be able to see where I'm going."

"Oh, Tony! What are we going to do? Look at the state she's in. How could someone break in and beat her up like this?"

"We'll worry about that later. Is the front door damaged? If it is, can you ask the neighbour to keep an eye on the place until we get back?"

"I'll shoot round there while you put Carol in the car."

Tony struggled to get Carol in the vehicle.

For the first time in a long time, Lorne felt inadequate. She knocked on the neighbour's door. "Hello, Helen. It's me again. We're taking Carol to the hospital. Could I ask a favour?"

"Yes. If there's anything I can do to help, you only have to ask."

"The front door has been damaged. I'll ring the police en route. Would you mind sitting in the house until they show up?"

"Absolutely. Is Carol all right?"

"Someone broke in, took some of her jewellery and battered her over the head. She was already suffering from a migraine and is in terrible pain. She passed out on us at the top of the stairs. Thanks so much for your help."

"Go. Not at all. It's a pleasure to help out. Send Carol my regards when she comes around, if you would."

"I'll do that. Help yourself to a cuppa. I'm sure Carol won't mind."

"I'll be fine. Stop fretting about me and rush her to the hospital."

Lorne nodded and raced up the path to the car. Tony started the engine, and Lorne slipped into the passenger seat beside him. She rang nine-nine-nine and reported the incident. Then she sent a text message to Charlie telling her what had happened. Her mobile rang not long after Lorne had hit the Send button.

"Mum, what the hell is going on?"

"Oh, Charlie. It was awful. Nathan dropped us off at the end of the street. We called at the pharmacy and then walked back to the house. The neighbour was standing at the front door. It was open. Carol has been battered over the head. Someone broke in, stole some of her jewellery, and then clouted her. She's passed out on the back seat now. We're taking her to A and E to get her checked over. I've rung nine-nine-nine and reported the crime. Helen, one of the neighbours, is sitting in the house now. I wondered if you could arrange for someone to fix the door for Carol from your end."

"Don't worry, I'll action it. I'll call SOCO to attend the scene, too. Send her my love and give her a gentle hug from me."

"I will and thanks, love. I'll be in touch when I know more."

"Take care."

Lorne ended the call and sighed heavily. She twisted in her seat to see if Carol was awake. She wasn't. She was dead to the world. Lorne reached through the seats and checked her friend's pulse.

"What's it like?" Tony asked.

"It seems normal, although I'm not an expert. Poor Carol, she doesn't deserve this."

He patted her thigh. "I know she doesn't. We'll soon be there. I don't suppose you've got your warrant card with you, have you?"

"No. I left it at home. Assumed I wouldn't be needing it. I'll tell them I'm a copper. They can always ring the station and ask Charlie."

"Let's hope that works, otherwise we could be waiting in A and E for hours."

After weaving in and out of the traffic, Tony finally drew up outside the A and E Department entrance. Lorne rushed inside to ask for assistance. A porter and a nurse followed her out to the car. The porter assisted Tony in getting Carol out of the back seat.

"I'll park the car and catch up with you."

Lorne had to run to keep up with the stretcher. Carol was rushed through to triage, and Lorne was blocked from entering.

"Take a seat. The doctor will have a chat with you after your friend has been assessed," the nurse said.

Tony entered through the door behind her and raced towards Lorne. They hugged each other and sat in the hallway. That's when the tears started to flow.

"There, there. She'll be all right. Carol is strong. She'll pull through this," Tony assured her.

"I hope so. To think, earlier all she had to worry about was having a migraine, and now this. What if the perpetrator has caused some real damage to her skull? The amount of blood that was pouring out of her wound doesn't bode well, does it?"

"Let's leave the speculation for now and hope the doctor comes and gives us an update soon."

It was a full hour before that happened. Lorne was pacing the hallway when a young male doctor came to speak to them. "I'm Doctor Napier. Your friend is stable. We've cleaned up the wound—no real damage done there. She's complaining about having a sore head, which is understandable in the circumstances. I'm proposing we admit her overnight to keep a close eye on her."

"She's had a migraine for the past couple of days. I'd just bought her some medication for it. When we got back to the house, we found someone had broken in. It's such a relief to know that she's going to be okay. Can we see her?"

"The porter will be moving her to a ward soon. You're welcome to accompany him if you like."

"Thank you, Doctor."

He smiled and returned to the triage area.

Lorne hugged Tony hard. "I'm so relieved she's going to be okay. I'd better text Charlie and let her know. She'll be worried sick about Carol."

"Aren't we all? Do you want a coffee?"

"Maybe when we get to the ward. The porter might appear with her any second."

As if on cue, a bed was pushed towards them. Carol smiled but closed her eyes instantly to block out the bright lights. She held up a hand for Lorne to take. "I'm sorry to put you through this."

"What are you talking about? Don't be daft. How are you feeling?"

"Ask me in a week's time. My head is pounding. They've given me a strong painkiller but warned me it might take a little while to work its way around my system."

"Hang in there."

"Do you want to come up to the ward with us?" the porter asked.

"Yes, please. If you don't mind?"

"Feel free."

They set off towards the lift. The porter called for it, and by the time the bed was loaded, it was a tight squeeze to fit them all in.

Carol was settled onto the ward a few minutes later. The nurse told them that they were allowed to visit for as long as Carol wanted them there. Within ten minutes, Carol was fast asleep and gently snoring. Lorne and Tony decided to leave her to get some much-needed rest, which in turn would help her heal quicker.

Lorne left her phone number with the nurse. "We're her good friends; she doesn't have any family, as such. We're staying with her at the moment. Can you call me when she wakes up?"

"I'll do that, but I think she's going to be out for the count for a while."

"I figured as much. Thank you. We'll drop in this afternoon, just in case."

"Very well."

There was a small Costa coffee shop close to the main entrance. Tony felt it would be a good idea for them to stop off there for a quick coffee before they got on the road again. He ordered the drinks, and Lorne sat at the table and rang Charlie.

"Hi, sweetheart. We're just having a breather before we head back to the house."

"How's Carol? Are they keeping her in?"

"Yes. The doctor doesn't think any real damage has been done. She woke up and complained that her head was hurting. I made him aware that she already had a migraine. Any news on SOCO?"

"Yes, I chased them up a little while ago. They're at the house. They reckon a crowbar had been used to get through the front door. I've sent the handyman from the station over there to see if there's anything he can do as a temporary fix. She'll probably need to get a new door fitted, which will be costly."

"I'll let her know. She should be able to claim back the expense from her insurance company. I'm relieved that it's been proven that someone broke in. I feared the worst. Thought that when we left this morning, we hadn't secured the door properly."

"How long are they keeping her in for?"

"The doctor reckons an overnight stay will put her on her feet again."

"Are we still on for going out tonight?"

"Can I get back to you once we assess the damage and determine if the door can be fixed? I'd hate to leave the house empty if it's not going to be safe."

"I understand. I'll let Nathan know, just to prewarn him. How did the viewings go, by the way?"

"One property was okay; the other one, we warned him to steer clear of, as it's bound to be a money pit. Plus, it was in a bad area, compared to the first option. He's going to have a word with the estate agent."

"How did you guys get on?"

Lorne sensed a note of hesitation in her daughter's tone. "Great. I think you've chosen well for yourself there, love."

"Aww… that's good to hear. I'm sorry I kept our relationship from you and Tony. I hope you understand that I needed to figure out if he was the right one for me or not."

"We completely understand. Is it the money? Is that what's concerning you?"

"Yes and no. You know how devoted I am to my career. Sometimes I feel blokes don't get it."

"I agree. It can put an unnecessary strain on a relationship. Although, saying that, I'm not getting the impression that it makes any difference to Nathan. He's head over heels in love with you, any fool can see that."

"Don't, you're making me blush."

"The question is, are you in love with him?"

"I think so. I have a strange feeling in my tummy, which is kind of alien to me."

Lorne chuckled. "And so it begins."

"I'm worried about Carol. We don't get many break-ins during daylight hours, as you know."

"Well, we don't in Norfolk. I did wonder if that would be the case down here these days. I'm going to knock on a few houses, ask if anyone saw anything."

"Good luck with that. You'll only have joy if all her neighbours are retired and at home all day."

"There's only one way to find out. I'll do that then we have to nip out to the shops to pick up some outfits."

"Oh, Mum, don't go too mad. I'm only going to wear a pair of black trousers and a sparkly top."

"Thanks for the heads-up. Are you nervous about meeting Nathan's mother?"

"I haven't had time to be. A new investigation came our way, so

Katy and I have been up to our necks in it all morning. Actually, the whole team has. I've got to go; Katy needs me. I'll tell you all about it later."

"Okay, good luck. You've got this."

"Thanks, Mum. I hope you find something suitable to wear for this evening. Promise me you won't spend too much. I know money is tight for you at the moment."

"Don't worry about us. Tony says he's got a bit stashed away."

"Lucky girl." Charlie blew a kiss down the phone.

Lorne ended the call. "Drink up, we should go."

They rushed back to the house, when they got there, Tony asked, "Everything okay with Charlie? You never said."

"Sorry, I got distracted. Yes. Charlie couldn't talk much because a new investigation has come their way today."

"Did she say what it was?"

"No, Katy needed her, so our call was cut short. Can you find out how the repairs are going?"

"He looks as though he's almost finished."

"Good. I'm going to knock on a few doors and ask the neighbours if they saw anything."

"That makes sense. Do you want me to help? We'll get the job done in half the time, leaving us free to get on the road again."

"Good idea. We can keep an eye on the handyman at the same time."

Lorne took a few of the houses on the right, and Tony made his way to the nearest neighbours on the left. They met back at Carol's ten minutes later, none the wiser. Some of the neighbours were out, and the others all told them that they hadn't seen anything.

"That's a bugger. I was hoping we would get a possible lead to pass on to the local police, but nothing." Lorne's shoulders slumped in defeat.

Tony put a finger under her chin and raised her head to look at him. "Don't give up. We'll get the bastard, I promise you."

"Sorry to interrupt," the handyman said from the doorway. "All finished now. Do you want to check it before I leave?"

Tony went with him while Lorne nipped to the toilet. When she came down again, the handyman had gone and so had the SOCO techs.

"Are you ready?" Tony asked.

"I am. How's the door now?"

"He's made a good job of it. Let's go."

TWO HOURS LATER, they returned to the house loaded with bags, as Tony had insisted on having a spend up for both of them.

"You've spoilt me rotten. Thank you. I'll dump these upstairs and then I'm going to call the hospital and see how Carol is. You look tired. Is your leg okay?"

He smiled. "You know me so well. I'll make a drink, and then I think I'm going to have a lie down for a bit, if that's all right with you."

"Tony, you don't have to ask my permission. Why don't you go up and I'll make the drink?"

"Deal, I'll take the bags up."

Lorne's heartstrings tugged. She hated to see him look so tired. *Maybe I should call the meal off or at least postpone it until tomorrow?*

"And don't even think about cancelling this evening," he shouted, reading her mind.

She laughed. "Who knows who well?"

"I'll be fine after a short rest. Anyway, we have to show off our new clothes, otherwise we'll have wasted our money for nothing."

"Okay, you win." She rang the hospital and spoke to the nurse they'd seen on the ward. "Hi, can you tell me how Carol is doing?"

"She's still asleep. The doctor has been around and examined her wounds. They're doing well. He told me that he'd given her some strong medication in the hope that she would sleep for the rest of the day. Carol had informed him that she hadn't been sleeping very well for a while. We'll keep a close eye on her throughout the afternoon and evening. Maybe you could visit her tomorrow?"

"Yes, I agree; that would be for the best. If she should wake up and need to speak to me, I'm here for her."

"I'll pass on the message. Enjoy the rest of your day."

"Thank you."

Lorne placed her phone on the worktop, filled the kettle and prepared the mugs. She glanced out at the birds sitting on the windowsill and looked in the bread bin to see if there were any spare slices she could throw out for them. The birds flew away as soon as she opened the door but came back once she had scattered the crumbs on the table. She left them to it and returned to the kitchen to watch them devour their treat.

She made the drinks and took them upstairs, only to find Tony snoring peacefully on the bed. She covered him with the blanket from the bottom of the bed and left him to rest.

Back downstairs, she sat on the sofa and sipped her coffee while contemplating what the evening ahead would hold for them. Before long, she found it impossible to keep her eyes open, so she put her feet up and grabbed forty winks.

4

Tony woke her up about an hour later with a fresh mug of coffee. "Looks like we both needed a nap."

"I had no intention of going to sleep, but as soon as I sat down, I struggled to keep my eyes open. Do you feel better now?"

"I'm fine. There's no need for you to worry about me. We should have this, then think about getting ready for this evening."

Lorne dropped her legs to the floor, allowing him to sit beside her. He hooked an arm around her shoulders, pulling her in for a cuddle.

"I wish we didn't have to go out tonight, but I think curiosity will get the better of me," Lorne said.

"That makes two of us. I wonder what she's like."

"Hard to imagine the type of woman who single-handedly brings up a young man and sets him up in the world. She must be so proud of what he's achieved so far. I just hope she's all right with Charlie. You know what some mothers are like with their sons."

"Yes, overprotective. Aren't you glad you didn't have that issue with my mother?"

She rested her head against his chest. "I would have loved to meet her. Do you still think about her?"

"Not as often as you think about your father. I secretly watch you sometimes and just know that you're reminiscing and thinking about him."

"You're right. He was a huge part of my life. I miss him every day."

He kissed her on the top of the head, and tears clouded her vision. "He was a massive influence on your life."

They received a text from Nathan that had been forwarded via Charlie's phone, giving them the location of the restaurant, which turned out to be about twenty minutes from the house.

"You look beautiful," Tony said as she descended the stairs. "Not that you don't look stunning every day," he added quickly.

"You redeemed yourself nicely there. You look very smart and handsome yourself."

Tony had treated himself to his first suit in years. It was mid-grey. A new white shirt and dark-grey tie completed his ensemble. He held out a hand and made Lorne do a twirl in the hallway. She'd decided on a red dress that wasn't too fancy and could be worn during the day as well as the evenings in the future.

"Stunning. I'm proud to be your husband."

Her cheeks reddened. "Don't go getting all mushy on me. I don't feel overly dressed in it. There's nothing worse than feeling uncomfortable and self-conscious in your clothes when meeting strangers."

"I agree."

Tony ensured the front door was locked properly and then opened the car door for Lorne.

They drove to the location in silence, each wrapped up in their own thoughts. In between getting changed and applying what little makeup she had with her, Lorne had called the hospital again, only to be told that Carol was still sleeping. She wouldn't have been able to enjoy herself this evening, knowing that her friend was awake and suffering.

"Penny for them? Are you thinking about Carol?"

"Yes. I'm glad she's still sleeping. Hopefully she'll be fully recovered by tomorrow and they'll allow her to come home."

"Do you want to consider staying on for an extra few days?"

"Would you mind?"

"Not at all. I think it makes sense. We can make sure she's back to her old self again before we head home. It would put your mind at rest, wouldn't it?"

"It would. Thanks, Tony, you're amazing."

"Let's hope Abby won't be too put out about the new arrangements."

"That's the problem. We're relying on putting other people out. Maybe we should sit on our plans for now. We can discuss it again as and when Carol is discharged."

"We're here now. Let's worry about that later and enjoy ourselves this evening. Stay there." He rushed around the front of the car and opened the door for her. "Let's do this properly."

"You crack me up. I wonder if they're here yet."

"There's one way to find out."

They entered the restaurant, and Tony told the woman on reception that they were meeting Nathan Cole.

"Ah, yes. Mr Cole and his guests are already here. If you'd like to come this way." She led them through the large area to a secluded part near the back. "Your other guests have arrived, Mr Cole. May I take your coats?"

Lorne slipped off her jacket and handed it to the woman.

"The waiter will be with you shortly to take your drinks order."

Charlie shot out of her seat and kissed them both. "That colour really suits you, Mum, and you look rather dashing this evening, Tony. You should treat yourselves more often," she whispered in Lorne's ear, then kissed her again.

"You look wonderful, too, sweetheart. I hope we haven't kept you waiting too long. There was a bit of a holdup in the traffic a couple of miles away."

"No, we've only been here five or ten minutes ourselves," Charlie said. She returned to her seat and patted the banquette beside her. Sit here, Mum. Tony, you can sit next to Nathan's Mum."

Nathan rose and shook hands with Tony. "I'd like to introduce you both to my mother, Gillian. Mum, these are Lorne and Tony, Charlie's mother and stepfather."

The woman was more frail than Lorne imagined she would be. Her hair was a rich steel colour, beautifully coiffured.

She smiled at them. "It's so lovely to meet you both. I'm sure we're going to get on well together. Charlie tells me that you're a police officer, too, Lorne."

"Yes. Charlie surprised me by following in my footsteps. I had no inclination that was her plan up until the day she signed up."

"Really? You must be so proud of her."

"I am. We are as a family. She's doing exceptionally well, already a sergeant at her age, which is no mean feat."

Nathan sat next to his mother, and she grasped his hand.

"I always knew Nathan would do well in his choices. I'm not talking about his career either. He's had a few girlfriends over the years but never one as down to earth as Charlie." She leaned in and said, "I must confess, I was dreading this evening."

"Mother!" Nathan chastised. "Don't tell them that. What are you like?"

"Why not? I'm only being honest. I think it's a good idea to be open and upfront with people, don't you, Lorne?"

"I do. It's the way I prefer to be with people."

The waiter arrived and took their drinks order. Nathan requested to have a bottle of champagne after their meal to celebrate their engagement, as well as several bottles of red wine while they ate.

"All that booze. I hope we don't get pulled over by the cops on the way home," Tony joked.

"You won't drink much, will you?" Lorne whispered in his ear.

"Don't be silly. Of course I won't. My licence means as much to me as it does to you."

"Good."

"So, what have you been up to since I dropped you off?" Nathan asked, directing his question at Lorne.

"It's been a mixed bag this afternoon. Not wishing to put a downer on the evening, but when we returned to our friend's house, we found her badly injured and had to rush her to the hospital."

"What? How did she get injured?" Nathan asked, "Did she have a fall?"

"No, someone broke into her house and stole some of her jewellery. They smacked her over the head at the same time. Whether they intended to hurt her or just knock her out, we don't know."

"Oh dear. I'm sorry to hear about your friend. What's the prognosis for her?" Gillian asked.

The woman seemed genuinely concerned, which Lorne appreciated. "They're keeping her sedated for now. She's had a migraine for the past few days and hasn't been sleeping well. The doctor felt this was the best thing for her to aid her recovery."

"I agree with the doctor," Charlie said. "Poor Carol. I've been worried about her all afternoon. Distracted from the case I've been working on."

Gillian rubbed her hands together. "Ooo, do tell, dearest Charlie. What sort of case is it?"

"Mother!" Nathan chastised his mother a second time.

Charlie put her hand over Nathan's and smiled. "It's fine. We were alerted to the possible abduction of a young estate agent called Davina Sedge."

Nathan's head shot round. "What's her name again?"

Charlie frowned. "Davina Sedge. Why? Do you know her?"

He ran a hand over his mouth and nodded. "I'm not sure if it's the same girl who I went to university with, but I knew a Davina Sedge back in the day."

"Sedge isn't a very common name," Lorne admitted. "It's probably the same girl."

"Thank you, Mother," Charlie said. "Have you seen or heard from her since you left uni?"

"University, dear, not uni," Gillian corrected to her son's amazement.

"Don't do that, Mother. Uni is fine."

An uncomfortable silence descended over the table. The waiter showed up with their drinks, extending the silence.

"To answer your question, no, I've not seen or heard from her in nearly eight years. Have you got any clues about what might have happened to her?"

"I don't want to dominate the evening, discussing work matters," Charlie said. She glanced sideways at Lorne.

"It's an ongoing case that you shouldn't really talk about in public, darling."

"Damn. I was hoping to get some inside gossip about what happened during an investigation," Gillian said.

"Mother!" Nathan warned for a third time. "I hope Davina is found soon. It's deplorable the way women go missing and are never seen again in this country. There are a lot of depraved individuals out there. I feel blessed to have people like you and your mother in a position of power to combat such criminals."

Lorne giggled. "Hardly a position of power. We're just doing our job, aren't we, Charlie?"

"Yes. Every police officer sets out to right the wrongs in this country."

Nathan raised an eyebrow. "Can you categorically tell me that's the truth, Charlie? The only reason I'm asking is because of all the current shit the Met is going through right now. Case upon case of corruption against high-ranking officers. The misogyny that has been reported on every news station throughout the country. I fear that when the public hear the stories and stats, their confidence in our police force could dwindle, and who could blame them?"

Lorne was shocked to hear his thoughts. It didn't matter that his words held a truth she'd often considered herself over the years—a notion that had led her to resign from her career on more than one occasion.

"Umm... I think we should talk about something else," Charlie said. She picked up her glass of wine and proposed a toast. "To our families joining together."

Everyone else raised their glasses and said the same.

They perused the menu, and Lorne and Tony chose the pâté to start with, followed by the chicken in a white wine sauce. The meal was delicious. The discomfort quickly eased around the table, and everyone appeared to be getting on. Well enough for Lorne to let herself relax, and she pushed any thoughts she had of Carol out of her mind. Once they had eaten their main courses, Gillian excused herself from the table. Lorne gave her a few seconds and then followed her to the toilet.

The ladies' was empty when she got there, but one of the cubicles was closed. Lorne used the cubicle next door and did her business. When she opened the door to wash her hands, she found Gillian standing there in tears. "Oh my, Gillian. What's wrong?"

The woman seemed shocked to see her, quickly wiping away her tears and dabbing at her eyes, careful not to disturb her makeup. "Oh, silly old me. There's nothing wrong, Lorne. Just ignore me."

"What? How could I possibly do that when you're clearly upset? Come on, tell me what's going on."

"I can't. Nathan would kill me."

Lorne took a step back and stared at her. "Why? You haven't done anything wrong, have you?"

"No. I haven't, or at least, I don't think I have. We have a complex relationship. I shouldn't be discussing it, not really. This is supposed to be a joyful occasion. Let's not spoil it."

"Okay. If that's what you want. I'll give you my number. Call me anytime you need to chat."

"You're too kind. No, I'm fine. You have enough on your plate to worry about at the moment, what with your friend being in hospital. I do hope she makes a full recovery. She must have been petrified to be confronted by an intruder. Please, send her my best wishes." Gillian shuddered. "That has to be my worst nightmare: to wake up and find a criminal in my bedroom. It doesn't bear thinking about, does it?"

"I know. I felt guilty because we were the last to leave the house and I thought I hadn't closed the door properly, but when SOCO turned up, they reckoned the intruder had used a crowbar to gain access to the house."

"And this happened during the day?"

"Yes. Tony and I checked with the immediate neighbours. Unfortunately, no one saw or heard anything."

"That is a shame. It reflects the world we live in, doesn't it? People are too busy with their own lives to care about what happens to others."

Lorne shrugged. "I suppose that's right, most of the time. Anyway, Carol's in the best place for her, and the house is secure again."

"I was going to ask if you had repaired the damage."

"Yes, Charlie arranged for the handyman who works at the station to come out and do it for us."

"How wonderful. It's hard to find someone at short notice these days. Tradesmen, in particular, seem to be in short supply. Youngsters of today, Nathan included, find it far easier to make money without getting their hands dirty. Umm... please don't tell him I said that."

Lorne smiled and winked. "Your secret is safe with me. I have to agree with you. Luckily, where we live in Norfolk, being rural, the opposite is true."

"Maybe it's only city boys who refuse to get down and dirty when it's needed, then."

"Are you all right now?"

"Yes. Sorry for making a fool of myself. Thank you for caring; it means a lot to me. I'm delighted we're going to be related soon. From what I've seen of Charlie so far, I think she'll be a super influence on Nathan. He needs a woman who is grounded and won't run home to Daddy every time they have an argument."

Lorne laughed at the image that conjured up in her mind. "I don't think there's any chance of that happening with Charlie."

"Is her father still around? May I ask how long you've been divorced?"

"He's around. He has certain issues that he's trying to combat, shall we say? Gosh, now you're asking; we've been divorced around fifteen years, I think. Please don't hold me to that. I'm not one for keeping a note of important dates."

"And time flies by as we get older. I can vouch for that. You seem happy enough with Tony."

"I couldn't be happier. We're true soulmates."

"How did you meet?"

Lorne wrinkled her nose. "Umm... during a very dangerous time in our lives." She decided to leave the facts scarce for now, not wishing to bore the woman further. She was also conscious of the time they had spent in the toilet away from the others.

"Maybe we can meet up for coffee sometime in the future, and you can run through the dynamics of what makes your family tick."

"We'll see. We'd better get back or the others will think we've run off and deserted them."

"Oh yes. You're probably right. I like you, Lorne. You have such a pretty name."

"Thank you. I'm not sure where my parents dug it up from. I've only ever heard about one other Lorne. She was an antiques expert on the TV a few years back."

"I'll have to do some research. I like doing that sort of thing. I did my family tree a few years ago. The less said about that, the better."

Intrigued, Lorne asked, "Oh, what secrets did you unearth?"

They left the toilet and made their way back to the table.

"I'll tell you another time, perhaps when we meet up for that coffee in the future."

"That would be great. It's something I've always considered doing —maybe when I retire for good."

"For good?"

"It's a long story, something to add to our conversation in the future."

"You're an interesting woman, Lorne."

"We were about to send out a search party to come and find you," Tony quipped.

"Sorry, we got chatting and forgot the time," Lorne admitted.

Gillian raised her glass and said, "To old friends and new.

Welcome to our family, Lorne and Tony. This evening has been an absolute pleasure. Now, where's the dessert menu?"

They chinked their glasses and laughed.

"Fancy going halves with me?" Lorne whispered in Charlie's ear.

"I don't think that's the done thing in a place like this, Mum. Just order something and leave what you can't manage; Nathan won't mind."

"Are you sure? I hate to waste food."

Charlie rolled her eyes. "I'm sure."

They settled on a chocolate fondant each, and the centre oozed out of the middle of the sponge. It was decadent and luscious, and despite not feeling that hungry, Lorne finished her dessert.

At the end of the evening, Gillian ended up drunk, and Lorne felt a little tipsy herself.

"I'm going to have to take Mother home. She can't be trusted getting a taxi in that state." Although Nathan said it light-heartedly, there was something in his tone that told Lorne he was a tad embarrassed by his mother's behaviour. "Tony, would you mind dropping Charlie home for me?"

"Of course not. That's fine by us, isn't it, Lorne?"

"Absolutely."

Tony offered to pay something towards the bill, but Nathan seemed offended by the suggestion.

"This was my idea. It's only right that I should pay for it."

Tony raised his hands. "I'm not one for arguments. Thank you for your kindness, Nathan."

"No, thank you for your expert advice earlier. One good turn and all that."

They left the restaurant.

Nathan clutched his mother's arm and steered her towards his car.

"Tony, you'd better lend a hand; she'll have trouble getting in that thing, like I did," Lorne said.

Tony held back and helped support Gillian while Nathan wrestled to get her into the passenger seat.

"Let's leave them to it." Lorne tucked her hand through Charlie's arm, and they got in Tony's car. "I thought the evening went well. Do you like Gillian?"

"She seems okay. Although I think you spent more time talking to her than I did. What did she have to say?"

"It was a bit awkward in the toilet to begin with."

"Why?" Charlie asked as she settled into the back seat.

"She was crying."

"What? Did she say why?"

"No, I couldn't get it out of her. She perked up a bit while I was talking to her. That's why we were so long in there."

"Wow. I wonder what that was about. Oh no, do you think it had to do with me? Maybe she doesn't like me."

"Don't be silly. I don't think that's the case at all. She was fine once we started talking. She wanted to know the ins and outs of a duck's arse. Asked me all about your father and how long we'd been divorced."

"I suppose she was intrigued about Dad, what with him not being there. I couldn't risk asking him, Mum. I'm sure the evening would have been an utter disaster if he'd been there."

"It's better to err on the side of caution where your father is concerned. Here's Tony now."

Tony opened the door and eased himself into the driver's seat. "That was fun. She was like a rag doll, flopping all over the place. Fair play to Nathan for keeping his cool with her. I'm not sure I would have if it had been my mother drunk as a skunk."

They all laughed.

"Are you fit to drive? How many did you have in the end?" Lorne asked.

"One and a half glasses. I'm glad Nathan decided against opening the champers. Can you imagine what his mother would have been like with that inside her?"

"Yeah, I'd rather not think about that," Charlie said. "Thanks for this evening, both of you. It made a change for us to be together."

"We enjoyed ourselves. I think it turned out to be the distraction we needed after what happened with Carol."

"When was the last time you rang her, or should I say contacted the hospital? Sorry, that was me being lazy. It's been a long day."

"Not the best day for a night out, eh?"

"No. However, Nathan was adamant we should celebrate tonight."

"You shouldn't let him get his way all the time," Lorne warned.

"I don't usually. We weren't sure how long you'd be staying, though."

"Ah, yes. That depends on how well Carol recovers. Sorry, you did ask, and I didn't answer. I rang before we left the house. The nurse told me she was still asleep due to the medication. I think it's the best thing for her."

"I hope she's going to be all right. What will we do without Carol around to guide us?"

"Let's not think about it, love."

Not long after, Tony drew up outside Charlie's house.

"Do you want to come in for a coffee?" Charlie asked.

"We'll decline if you don't mind. You look tired. You should get your rest if you have a new investigation to work on in the morning."

"If you're sure." She leaned through the gap and gave them both a kiss. "I'll give you a call during the day. But if you hear anything about Carol, will you ring me to let me know?"

"Of course we will. We'll sit here until you're safely inside the house," Lorne said.

"I'm not a teenager. Thanks again for a lovely evening. Sleep well."

"You, too."

They waited until Charlie entered the house, then Tony drove back to Carol's.

"Are you going to tell me what went on in the toilet between you and Nathan's mother?"

"I wish I knew. She was in tears. I got talking to her, and she seemed okay after a while. I was afraid that she didn't like us or Charlie, but I needn't have worried on that front. Maybe she was just overwhelmed by the evening and what it meant to her and her family. It's not every day your wealthy son gets engaged."

"Ouch, why do you keep calling him *wealthy*? I got the impression there was more to him than just the money. I don't think he's the type to throw it down our throats all the time. Do you?"

"I'm on the fence. Don't get me wrong, he's a nice enough bloke... I suppose I'm being cautious for Charlie's sake. I hope he's not expecting her to give up her career because that will cause trouble between them. Charlie is adamant she wants to work her way up the ladder. She's smart enough to do it, as well."

"Charlie has got her own mind. Any man can see that. It would be foolish for anyone to try to change her."

"I agree. All in all, I thought it was an enjoyable, relaxing evening. I didn't feel uncomfortable in the slightest. Well, apart from finding his mother in tears, but we soon overcame that issue."

"I agree. It was a very successful evening. Just a shame Carol wasn't well enough to join us. I would have loved to get her take on Nathan and his mother."

"There will be time for that in the future."

5

He thumped the steering wheel, fuming that he had missed his opportunity by arriving late at the scene. His relief came when the woman he was waiting for left the gym. It was a great idea, trialling the gym to be open twenty-four hours a day. Whether it would work out to be something the locals welcomed and used was another matter entirely. He pulled the rubber mask into place, exited the car and pretended to walk casually towards the building. He was aware of where the cameras were so kept his distance from them. His intention was not to move too far from his vehicle, as it was an essential part of his plan.

The woman with long blonde hair glanced over her shoulder. She seemed anxious as he got closer to her. She lowered her head to avoid eye contact. There was a chill in the air, but you wouldn't think so given the way she was dressed. He needed to rid his mind of all that crap and concentrate on the job in hand.

She passed him. He mumbled a hello which she ignored. While she was within feet of him, he grabbed her arm, tugged her towards him and shoved a hand over her mouth.

"One scream, and I'll kill your family. I know where they live."

Her eyes widened. She shook her head.

He had the impression she didn't believe him, so he reeled off her mother's address. "Forty-eight Hardacre Road. I know what time she leaves for work, where she works, and what time she returns every day. Are you going to behave, or are you willing to risk the lives of your mother and little sister?"

She shook her head again.

"That's a good girl. You're going to walk with me, arm in arm. I'm going to remove my hand now. One scream, and I'll break your neck. Then I'll drive to your mother's house and kill her and your sister. Got that?"

She nodded.

He released his hand and linked arms with her, then steered her back towards his vehicle. He placed her in the passenger seat and put clear tape over her mouth, just in case a copper drew up alongside them at the lights on their journey back. She allowed him to do it without putting up any resistance.

He jumped into the driver's seat and patted her thigh. "See, I knew you'd be compliant. You women learn quickly when a member of your family is at risk."

She said something that he couldn't quite understand because of the tape stretched over her mouth.

"Save it until we get to our location. It's not too far. You'll be pleased when we get there, I promise. There's a surprise waiting for you."

She stared at him, her eyes still as wide as saucers.

He laughed and started the engine, then drew out of the parking space. It wasn't long before he reached the location. This time, he chose to keep the tape in place. "We're going to play this out the same way. I'm going to come round and accompany you up the path to the house. If you attempt to run or cry out for help, you know what will happen."

She nodded. He opened the door and ran around the front. He helped her out of the vehicle, held on to her arm, and then guided her up the path. He opened the door with his key and, keeping the tape in place, walked her through the hallway to the cellar.

She shook her head.

He nodded. "Oh, yes. Don't worry, you won't be alone."

He forced her to descend the stairs in front of him. She faltered slightly, so he nudged her. She almost lost her footing and peered over her shoulder to glare at him.

He wagged a finger. "Don't even go there. Behave, or suffer the consequences—the choice is yours, sweetheart. I've got better things to do with my time than keep repeating myself."

They reached the bottom of the stairs in one piece. He took a step towards her and tore off the tape. She winced and rubbed at her lips.

"Take off your clothes."

"What? Why? No, please, don't do that…"

He tutted and crossed his arms. "Did you not hear me? I said I don't appreciate having to repeat myself. Now, do as you're told or…"

"No, you don't have to say it again."

"Why are you holding us here?" the other girl said.

"Umm… let me think about that for a moment or two. Ah yes, because I can. I don't need any other excuse or reason for doing this." He held up his hands. "I have the power, which I intend to use. Don't worry, you won't be the only ones I punish." He sneered, and the woman retreated a few steps. "Now, you're trying my patience. Do what I say, and you won't get hurt. Refuse… and I'll break your fingers, one by one."

The woman slowly removed her clothes. He crossed the room and collected a hessian sack from the stack on the chair. She got down to her underwear.

"Stop there. I'd rather not see your jiggly bits or that bush of yours. Put this on."

He threw it at her. The sack dropped to the floor because she wasn't quick enough to catch it. He slapped her hard around the face, and her head snapped to the right.

"Don't mess with me, woman. Try my patience once more, and I'll leave here and drive straight to your mother's. Are you really willing to take the risk?"

"No. Leave them out of this. Do what you want to me."

He took a step towards her and pressed his forehead against hers. "Thanks, but I don't need your permission. You'd be wise to remember that going forward. You need to be like Davina here: compliant and eager to please. How was your dinner this evening, Davina?" He glanced down at the empty plate by the door.

"It was nice. Thank you for feeding me."

"You're welcome. See, you could learn a lot from Davina. She knows how to treat me and knows which side her bread is buttered on."

"Good for her."

The sarcastic comment earnt her another slap. He pushed her back against the bars, his forearm cutting off the air to her throat. "Don't push me, I'm warning you. You won't like me when I'm angry."

He released his hold on her. She doubled over and started coughing.

"Don't exaggerate; it wasn't that bad."

She spluttered and gasped for breath. "I'm sorry. It won't happen again."

"It better not. Just so we're clear on this: I'm not in the habit of making idle threats. If I say I'm going to do something, I do it. That's your final warning. One more step out of line and... Hardacre Road, here I come."

"No, I won't. I promise. What do you want from us?"

"All will be revealed in good time. For now, I'll leave you and Davina in peace. She'll tell you, so far, I've treated her fairly. Saying that, she's given me the respect I deserve. You'd be wise to treat me the same way."

Davina reached through the bars and caught the new woman's arm. "We'll be safe together."

"Will we?"

"Finish dressing yourself," he said. "I have somewhere I need to be. Have you eaten?"

"Yes, I had a sandwich earlier this evening before I went to the gym."

"Is that advisable? Don't bother answering. I couldn't give a shit one way or the other. Put it on."

She slipped the sack over her head, and it rustled as it slid into position and covered her body. "It's scratchy on my skin, very uncomfortable."

"You'll get used to it," Davina assured her.

He unlocked the cell door and gestured for her to step inside. She hesitated for a second but thought better of it when he tutted and urged her to hurry up.

"Jesus, get on with it."

"Sorry. I don't want to be held in a cell."

"For fuck's sake, do you think you've got an option?"

His patience snapped. He pushed her into the cell. Davina caught her and put an arm around her shoulder. "Talk some sense into her, Davina." He closed the door then removed his mask.

The new woman gasped and slapped a hand over her mouth. She dropped it and said, "You? Why are you doing this?"

"Have a word with her, Davina. Tell her to stop asking such dumb questions."

He locked the door and let out a sinister laugh as he walked away and climbed the stairs. After sliding the bolt across and locking the door for extra security, he left the house and returned to his car, grinning and pleased with his accomplishments that evening. *Two down, only one more to go.* He rubbed his hands together, the excitement growing within.

6

Charlie drove to work the following morning with a slightly thick head, regretting having the three glasses of wine she'd consumed. After Nathan had dropped his mother home, he'd rung her. By that time, she was already in bed, exhausted from her busy day and the effort of putting on a show for his mother that evening. He'd wanted to return and spend the night with her, but she had persuaded him not to. He wasn't upset by her refusal; he just told her he loved her and that he'd see her soon.

At the traffic lights close to the station, she glanced at the rock sitting on her finger. She'd already decided that she would wear it for a few days at work and then leave it at home the rest of the time, not wanting to risk losing it during her working day.

A car horn sounded behind her, urging her to pay attention to the lights changing. She held up a hand to apologise to the vexed driver and drove off.

Outside the station, she parked next to Katy's spot. She was surprised to find it empty, given the time. Katy beeped and drew up alongside her. Charlie waved and waited for her partner on the pavement.

"Hey, how did it go last night?" Katy shouted as soon as she got out of the car.

"Can't you ask quietly?" Charlie rubbed her head.

"Ouch, sorry. You don't look hungover. I take it everything went well then, yes?"

"It did. We didn't get home too late."

"But you continued to party when you got home. Is that what you're telling me?"

"Hardly. I had three glasses of wine during the meal. Mum and Tony dropped me back to my house, while Nathan took his mother home."

"Not the end to the evening you were expecting by the sounds of it. What's up, Charlie?"

"Nothing. At least I think it's nothing. I need to check out a few things this morning."

"Such as."

"It might be nothing. I'd rather not say, just in case I end up with egg on my face."

"Hmm... sounds ominous. I'm dying to know now."

"One thing is definite: I'm going to need a gallon of our favourite drink to get me going this morning."

"Nothing new there."

They walked through the main doors to find the desk sergeant in a tizzy, organising his staff for the day. Katy and Charlie waved and opened the security door. When they reached the incident room, Katy prepared the coffee while Charlie switched on all the relevant computers in the office. Then she sat at her desk and began searching the internet for answers.

Katy handed the mug to her and peered over Charlie's shoulder. "Should I stick around or get on with my own chores?"

"The latter. This might take me a while to get to the answers I'm searching for."

"I'll leave you to it. Give me a shout when everyone's here. We'll hold the morning meeting and then crack on with the investigation."

Charlie raised her thumb, distracted by the information she had found on the screen.

Katy left her to it and entered her office.

Over the next ten minutes, the rest of the staff arrived. When everyone had poured themselves a drink and were at their desks, Charlie let Katy know.

Katy joined them and drew everyone's attention to the board. "So, what we need to do is follow up on what we uncovered yesterday. We still haven't spoken to the ex-boyfriend yet; let's make him our priority today. Does anyone have anything else they'd like to add?"

Charlie raised her hand. "I do."

Her colleagues turned to look at her.

"Go on. You've been very secretive since we got here this morning. Do you want to tell us all what you've been working on?"

"Okay. Last night I had a family dinner to celebrate my engagement to Nathan. During the evening, his mother asked me what sort of investigation I was working on. I didn't think anything about telling her; I'm sorry if I did the wrong thing. The interesting part is that when I mentioned Davina's name, Nathan told me he went to university with her."

"Get away! What a coincidence. So, you've been checking out the other pupils who were there at the same time, have you?"

"Yes. As yet, I haven't got very far on that. I just thought I should throw it into the mix."

"Thanks, Charlie. While you're digging, can you do me a favour and see if the boyfriend went to uni with Davina, as well?"

"Good call. I'll get back to it."

Charlie immediately found the photo of those who'd attended the year in question and rigorously checked through it. She found a list of the names and printed it off. She did the same for the next few years until Davina graduated. While she was doing this, something else caught her eye. She refreshed the page and went back and forth a couple of times, just to make sure that what she'd spotted was correct and not merely a figment of her imagination.

She sat back and stared at the wall.

Katy stopped by her desk and asked, "Is everything all right? You seem perplexed."

"Yes, I'm just working things out in my head. No sign of the boyfriend. Perhaps she met him when she started work."

"Okay, we'll keep searching for him. Are you sure you're okay?"

"Yes, I'm fine."

Katy worked her way around the room.

Charlie kept half an eye on what everyone was up to as she upped her research. It was an angle she hadn't considered the investigation veering off in. *Am I doing the right thing?* She felt deceitful, keeping Katy and the rest of the team out of the loop. But the direction her research had taken her in was nothing to do with the investigation. It was personal. And personal issues had no place at work. It was against the rules to carry out personal searches for someone you knew. However, despite the risk she was taking, Charlie felt drawn to continue with the task at hand.

She cast her mind back to a conversation she'd had with Nathan a few weeks before. He'd told her that he regretted the fact that his father hadn't been alive to see him graduate from Oxford. Except, from the research she had conducted, Nathan had never graduated from the university. He had lied to her.

Why would he lie to me? Christ, it wouldn't matter one way or the other if he'd graduated or not. He's a successful businessman, despite not having the degree behind him. But why had he lied to me?

She dug a little deeper into his family background and was shocked to find a photo of Nathan with his mother. She had to blink and rub at her eyes. The woman looking back at her on the screen wasn't Gillian. She inched forward to read the article. The woman was called Olivia.

What the fuck is going on here? Why the deception?

Katy's hand clasped her shoulder, scaring the crap out of her.

Charlie hit a button to clear her screen. "Do you have to sneak up on me like that?"

Katy laughed. "I thought you might have seen me heading your way. Are you all right? You've gone deathly white."

"No. I'm not feeling well. I need to go to the toilet." Charlie darted out of the room and bumped into two uniformed officers in the hallway. "Sorry for being so clumsy. It's an emergency."

The officers laughed. Charlie bolted through the door of the ladies'. She locked the cubicle and emptied her stomach down the toilet, then wiped the sweat from her brow. She stayed in the cubicle for the next couple of minutes, her mind reeling like a tornado. She had remained guarded all these years. Apart from Brandon, she had failed to let another man in, refusing to allow anyone to mess with her emotions. Why had she accepted Nathan's proposal? Why hadn't she thought about researching whether he was legit?

Because it had never occurred to me. Why would it? Up until now, I've had no reason to think he was lying to me. So why was he? What did he hope to achieve by deceiving me—and my family, come to that? Jesus, and who was the woman he brought to dinner last night? What's that all about? Why introduce her as his mother?

So many questions, and yet she couldn't think of a suitable answer to any of them.

What should I do? Keep digging? Confront him tonight when I get home? Tell Katy? Tell Mum and Tony?

The outer door opened, and heels clip-clopped on the tiles. "Charlie, are you in here?"

She flushed the loo again, straightened her skirt and jacket and opened the door. "Sorry, I had an upset tummy and…"

Katy held up her hand. "I think I can figure out the rest of that sentence myself. Are you sure you're fit enough for work?"

"Yes. Stop fretting about me. I'm fine now." She washed her hands and dabbed some cold water on her flushed cheeks.

"Who are you trying to convince? Because it's not working on me."

Charlie rolled her eyes. "I'll get back to work."

"No, you won't. That's why I came to look for you."

She turned to face Katy and tilted her head. "Why? What's up?"

"Another woman has been reported missing, close to where Davina vanished."

"What the fuck? What do we know about her?"

"She's called Isla Merrick. She runs a boutique, not far from the estate agents where Davina works."

"Who reported her missing?" Charlie asked.

"A member of her staff when she failed to show up for work."

"Is she married?"

"She's separated from her husband. So that's a lead we need to follow up on."

"And do we know when she went missing?"

"Overnight. The woman who reported the incident told the desk sergeant that she usually went to the gym on Thursdays around eleven."

Charlie frowned. "Why so late if she had work the next day?"

"I haven't got that far. Fancy a trip out to the boutique?"

"As if we haven't got enough to do," Charlie complained.

"You can pass over the research you were carrying out to someone else. I think it's important that we hit the ground running if we have a serial abductor in the area."

"Okay. I can deal with the other job later. I'd nearly completed the task. Seems pointless passing it on to someone else to do at this stage."

"I've also received some good news about the search that was carried out down by the canal. The team found a mobile, and we're assuming it's Davina's. They've sent it to the lab for testing."

"That is good news. What about her handbag or purse? Any sign of those?"

"No. Only the phone for now. We need to count our blessings."

They rushed back to the incident room to collect their coats. Charlie was still slightly distracted when they drew out of the car park, enough for Katy to ask again if she was okay.

"Honestly, I'm fine. Please stop mithering me."

"All right. There's no need for you to snap my head off. Pardon me for being concerned. You'd be the same if I were acting out of sorts."

"I know. I don't know what else to tell you."

"You would tell me if there was something wrong, wouldn't you?"

"Of course I would." Charlie turned to look out of the window to avoid Katy detecting the relief she felt.

They arrived at the boutique to find Fiona Watkins in tears.

Katy took the lead and introduced herself and Charlie to the wailing woman. "I'm DI Katy Foster, and this is my partner, DS Charlie Simpkins. Why don't you tell us what you know, Miss Watkins?"

She tore a tissue out of the box on the counter next to her and blew her nose. "I'm sorry. You must think I'm a right idiot, creating like this over my boss."

"Not in the slightest. I take it you're close to her?" Katy asked.

"Yes. She's the best boss ever. Isla is more like a sister to me. What do you want me to tell you?"

"If you wouldn't mind repeating what you told the desk sergeant when you reported her missing."

"Well, Isla usually goes to the gym later in the evening. I queried the time and why she preferred to go late at night, and she said it was because it was quieter. I suppose she had a point; most people who have to get up in the morning are probably in bed by then."

"And she frequently visits the gym?"

"Yes, every other day during the week, and if she doesn't have much on, she also goes there on a Saturday or Sunday, as well. She loves to keep fit."

"I have to ask, has she mentioned anything concerning her lately?"

"No, just the usual. She was complaining about the rates and the energy bills on this place skyrocketing but nothing else, not from what I can remember."

"You mentioned that she was separated from her husband. Is he aware of her routine?"

Fiona shrugged. "Possibly. Although I don't think he is. She started visiting the gym after she split up from him. She'd put on some excess weight in the wrong areas and was determined to shift it, hence her going there several times a week. Rather her than me. I tried it once and hated it, but then I'm a lazy bugger at the best of times."

"Did she visit the gym with a friend or alone?"

"Alone. She's very self-conscious about working out in front of other people. I felt the same when I went years ago. That's why I've never returned. Fiona had found a way to combat the embarrassment by attending the gym later at night."

"Did she talk about the visits she'd made there recently?"

"No. Only to tell me that her instructor thought she was doing well. She hadn't lost any weight, but she had gained muscle, which was her aim."

"Has she dated anyone since she split up with her husband?"

"No. She told me because of the rough ride she had with him, she needed time to get her emotions under control before she entertained going out with anyone else."

"A rough ride? Did he abuse her?"

"Yes. It was mostly verbal abuse until the time he laid a hand on her. That's when she said enough was enough and reported him to the police. They were brilliant and gave her some really useful advice, which she followed. She refused to leave the family home because she had been the one who had saved to put the deposit down on the house. Her husband never had a bean left at the end of the month, which ticked her off. I think that's where all the problems started within their marriage. She was fed up with handing over her hard-earned money to him to dig him out of a financial mess."

"Do you know where he is now?" Katy asked.

"At this moment? No."

"Sorry, what I should have asked was where he's living now."

"He's staying at a friend's place until he outstays his welcome."

"I don't suppose you have an address to hand, do you?"

"No, sorry. He works at a DIY store about five miles from here."

Katy glanced at Charlie, who was taking notes. "B and Q, is it?"

"That's right. He loads the lorries before they go out on deliveries."

"Thanks. We'll drop by and see him."

"Do you think he might be behind her going missing?"

"Possibly. He'd definitely be someone we'd be keen to speak to from the outset. I take it you've tried calling Isla's phone?"

"Yes. I tried last night and again this morning. She always rings me after the gym session. Well, every night before she goes to bed. She has done that since she split up from her husband. Mainly because she hates living alone. I'm always reassuring her, telling her that she's worrying about nothing, and now this has bloody happened. I feel guilty about that. She probably let her guard down because I'm always reinforcing upon her how safe she is. Please, you've got to find her. You hear all sorts about weirdos walking the streets. I can't believe this has happened to someone I know. To Isla. And if it's not Mike who is responsible, then I fear what will happen to her."

"Don't worry, we'll find her. It's great that you contacted us so soon after she went missing."

"Is it? I should have reported her missing last night when she failed to call me. I just thought she'd forgotten. I've been going out of my mind since first thing. I thought I'd check on her the second I woke up, but her phone is dead. Either that or someone has switched it off. She never turns her phone off. It's always charged, whether at home or here at work. She relies on it heavily as she hasn't got a landline at the house."

"That's good to know. We can try to trace it if you give us the number."

She scrolled through her mobile and slid it across the counter for Charlie to note down Isla's number.

"Thanks," Charlie said and pushed the phone back towards her. "Can you tell us the name of the gym?"

"I can look it up for you." She reached for her phone again and searched the internet. "Here it is: Twenty-Four Hours Fit."

Again, Charlie scribbled down the information.

"Has she mentioned being under stress lately? Maybe someone hanging around who you hadn't noticed?"

"No. Nothing like that at all. If anything, life has been treating her well, considering she kicked her husband out a few months ago. This has got to be down to him. I've never trusted the bastard—not that I would have told her that while she was still married to him. He's childish. The type who spits his dummy out of the pram if he doesn't get his way."

Katy nodded. "Interesting. Why did she marry him? Or is that a silly question?"

Fiona shrugged. "Why do women do a lot of things where their fellas are concerned? She was conned by him. He was all right until they got married, and then he changed. Maybe he duped her into thinking he was someone he wasn't, and as soon as they were married, he showed his true colours, like a lot of men do."

"That might be the case. We'll have to have a word with him. What's her demeanour been like of late?"

"Perfectly fine. The business has been doing really well." Fiona dipped her head.

"Are you okay?"

"Just sad. Upset more like. I can't stop thinking about what might be happening to her. She doesn't deserve this. There are only bad reasons coming to mind for why someone would abduct another person, aren't there?"

"We don't know she's been abducted yet. You'll be better off not thinking about it."

"How do you do that? I don't think I'm going to be able to." She dabbed at her eyes with the tissue.

"Try not to get yourself worked up about this. You've done the right thing by calling us. One last question before we go."

"What's that?"

"I don't suppose you can tell us if Isla knows a woman by the name of Davina Sedge?"

Fiona glanced up and frowned. "Yes. Davina passes by the shop every day on her way to work. She's an estate agent up the road. They're good friends. They went to Oxford together when they were younger and have remained friends ever since those days. Why?"

"I see. Because we believe Davina was abducted two nights ago."

"What the...? You're kidding me. I didn't know. Did Isla know?"

Katy shrugged. "I guess we have no way of knowing that, not until we find them both."

"This is too shocking for words. Someone must have targeted them in that case, mustn't they, if they knew each other? What are the odds of both of them going missing within a few days of each other if this wasn't planned?"

Katy nodded. "The thought had crossed my mind. Okay, if there's nothing else you can tell us, we need to get on with the investigation."

"Not trying to tell you how to do your job, but my first port of call would be that scumbag of a husband of hers."

"Don't worry, he's the first one on our list. Thanks for all your help."

They left the shop and marched back to the car.

"Do you think this is to do with the husband?" Charlie asked.

"Possibly. But it's too much of a coincidence, the friends going missing like this. We'll visit him and check out his alibi, but I'm not getting the impression he's involved."

"Because they're both missing and not just Isla?"

"Correct."

They drove to B and Q and asked to speak to Mike Merrick.

The girl at the reception desk made a call. "He'll be through in a moment. Can you step back? There's a lady waiting to be served behind you."

Katy and Charlie stood aside for the customer who was seeking a refund.

"How are you going to handle this?" Charlie murmured.

"I'm going to come right out and ask him. I don't think we've got time to beat around the bush, not with two women's lives in danger."

"You rang, Lisa?" a young man asked as he rounded the corner.

"These two ladies would like a word with you, Mike."

He frowned and approached them. His chin was sporting three to four days' growth, and his uniform was dirty and creased.

Katy and Charlie produced their warrant cards.

"DI Katy Foster and DS Charlie Simpkins. Is there somewhere we can have a chat in private?"

"Umm... not really. I mean, we've got a canteen, but people are in and out of there all day long. Have I done something wrong?"

"Is there a storeroom we could use?"

"What about the manager's office?" Lisa suggested once she'd finished dealing with the other customer. "He's popped out to another store for a few hours. He's not due back for a while yet."

"Thanks. That will do," Katy said.

Mike heaved out a breath. "You'd better come with me."

They followed him up the paint aisle to an office at the rear of the store that was quite small, considering it was the manager's.

"Take a seat, if you can find one. I prefer to stand." He crossed his arms and tapped his foot. "Before you start, I need to see your IDs. Let's face it, there are a lot of dodgy characters around these days. Better to be safe than sorry."

"I absolutely agree with you."

Katy and Charlie allowed him to study their IDs and then slipped them back into their pockets.

"Right, what can I do for you, ladies?" He leaned against the wall, his arms still folded.

"We'd like to have a chat with you about your wife, Isla."

He launched himself upright and dropped his arms to the sides. "What about her? She's nothing but a two-faced bitch. We had a future together, except we had to do things her way. I wasn't up for that and told her that marriage is supposed to be a partnership. She had problems with that part. I know she runs her own business and I'm a warehouse assistant but..."

Katy held a hand up to stop his verbal diarrhoea. "Please, calm down."

"If she's told you I've done something to her then she's a born bloody liar. I haven't been near her for a while. She told me she needed a breather. I've given her that. It's not easy sleeping night after night on someone's clapped-out couch, I can tell you."

"I can imagine. When was the last time you either saw or spoke to her?"

"About a month ago. Why? What's she said?"

"She hasn't told us anything. Did you see her in person or call her?"

"She rang me about getting a solicitor. She's divorcing me."

"You say that as though it came as a shock to you. Did it?" Katy asked.

"Too bloody right it did. I thought we were going to at least attempt to work things out. It was supposed to be a trial separation that went on for months."

"Why?"

"You tell me! She kept saying she needed more space to figure things out. I gave her the space she needed, then she hit me with the bombshell that she wanted to go ahead with the divorce. I don't want that, and I told her."

"What was her response?"

"She said it was tough, it's what she wanted." He shrugged again. "That's something I'm going to have to live with. I love her, but she told me she's fallen out of love with me because..."

"You abused her?"

His chin dropped on to his chest, and then he raised his head and tipped it back to look up at the ceiling. "I only hit her the once. It was a mistake. I apologised straight away, but by that time the damage had already been done. I pleaded with her to forgive me. She refused to. Told me that things had been building to a head for some time."

"And, had they?" Katy asked.

"Yes. I was frustrated. I took my bad mood out on her. I didn't mean to. That's what married people do from time to time, don't they?"

Katy shook her head. "No, it shouldn't be like that."

"Hark at you. Don't stand there and tell me you've never had a barney with your husband?"

"I haven't. We've had the odd disagreement, but he's never raised his hand to me."

"Because you're a frigging copper, that's why."

"No, I don't think that's the case at all. The reason is that he respects me too much to sink to that level."

He waggled his head and pulled a face. "Bully for you. You haven't told me why you're here. Has she reported me for hitting her?"

"No. Although that's not to say she shouldn't have. No man has the right to slap his wife around. It's classed as common assault these days, just for future reference."

"Don't worry, I've learnt from my mistake. So, why are you here?"

Katy watched his reaction when she told him the truth. "Your wife has been reported missing."

His head jutted forward, and his brow furrowed. "She what? When? Who reported her missing?"

"Fiona, who works with her at the boutique."

"When?"

"This morning. Where were you last night?"

"I was at my mate's place. Paddy can vouch for me. We were playing on his Nintendo all night."

"Until what time?"

"It was a late one. I think we went to bed at around midnight."

"Can you give us Paddy's phone number so we can corroborate that?"

He removed his phone from his pocket and dialled a number. "Here, you can speak to him."

Katy accepted the phone.

A man with an Irish accent answered. "I whipped your arse good and proper last night, man. What do you want? Are you calling up for a rematch?"

"Hello, this is Detective Inspector Katy Foster. Is this Paddy I'm speaking to?"

"Oh, right. Yes. What's going on? Where's me mate, Mike? And what are you doing with his phone?"

"It's okay. He's safe. I'm calling to see if you'll give him an alibi for last night."

"What's he need one of them for? What's he done wrong?"

"Nothing as far as we know. We're investigating a serious crime."

"Well, I'm telling you, Mike ain't got it in him. He was with me all night. We played video games until about one this morning."

"Thanks. That's all I need to know." Katy ended the call before Paddy could ask anything else.

Mike laughed. "I bet his mind will be working up a storm by now. He loves a good old gossip, that one."

"Can you tell us if Isla had been having problems with anyone before you left the marital home?"

"No. I don't think so. All she did was work, work, work at that boutique of hers, which ended up getting on my nerves. She always brought work home with her, despite our pact when we first got together that she wouldn't. Like everything in our marriage, it all changed once we started living together."

"Did she change or did you?"

"A bit of both. No one stays the same, not these days. Do you think I want to spend the rest of my life working in this shithole? I don't. I'm only using this as a stopgap. I had a good career in IT until I was made redundant a couple of years ago. Rather than sit at home complaining about it, I took the first job that came my way. I hate it here. And yes, accepting the job put a terrible strain on our relationship. My father always told me that it's easier to find work when you're already in a job."

"That's true. My father always says the same. Okay, I think we're done here. If Isla should contact you for any reason, will you give me a call and let me know?" Katy handed him a card.

"I will. I hope you find her soon. If you want me to join a search, I'll willingly do it after work."

"I don't think there will be any need for that, but thanks for the offer."

He saw them through the shop, and they parted at the reception desk.

"What did you make of him?" Charlie asked on the way back to the car.

"He seemed genuine enough. I think all he's guilty of is having a short fuse. Given the circumstances, working in a job that he hates, I suppose we have to make an exception for him."

"I thought you let him off lightly. That's not a criticism by the way."

Katy laughed. "I'm glad to hear it. We have to judge every situation as we find it. I felt he was a man down on his luck. I put myself in his shoes and shrugged it off. I think I'd be frustrated as well, losing a job I loved and taking on one that I hated just to keep the money rolling in."

"When you put it like that," Charlie replied. "Where are we going now?"

"We've got the other boyfriend to chase up while we're out and about."

THEY RETURNED to the station an hour later, unable to track down Davina's former boyfriend.

"I'm getting the impression that he doesn't matter anyway," Katy announced to the team. "Our priority is to check what other connections Davina and Isla have. We need to search through their latest SM posts and see if anything shows up there. What we know so far is that they attended Oxford together. Maybe there's something in their past that has been lingering since then and has only just come to the surface."

Charlie stared at her screen. After Katy drew the meeting to a close, she stopped by Charlie's desk to see if she was all right.

"You've gone quiet all of a sudden. I thought you were feeling better?"

"I'm all right. Just sitting here thinking. I'll crack on and search a few of the other SM accounts rather than the more popular ones."

"I'm going to chase up the lab and ask if they've had a chance to work on Davina's phone yet. We might glean something from her messages or her searches."

"Great idea."

"Chin up. We'll get the breakthrough we need soon, I'm sure of it."

Charlie held up her crossed fingers.

FRUSTRATED, Katy dismissed the team at around six that evening. "Are you okay?" she asked Charlie once they were in the car park.

"Nothing an early night won't put right. I'll see you in the morning."

"Wait, aren't you seeing your mum and Tony tonight?"

Charlie's shoulders slumped. "I wasn't planning to. I'll give them a call when I get home. I need to find out how Carol is getting on, anyway."

"Send them my love."

"Send mine to AJ and Georgie, too. Enjoy your evening, Katy."

"Let's hope we get the investigation moving in the right direction tomorrow. Have a good rest this evening. Take care."

Charlie rang her mum on the way home. "Hey, sorry I haven't been in touch today—we've been here, there and everywhere. How is Carol doing?"

"Hi, you don't have to apologise, darling. I totally understand what's involved when a new investigation comes your way."

"It's not just that. Another woman has gone missing. She's friends with the first victim, so there's something more sinister going on than we first anticipated."

"Oh bugger. That doesn't sound good. I hope you find them both soon. I'm on my way to visit Carol now. They left her to sleep all day."

"Poor Carol. Send her my love when you visit her."

"I will. You sound weary, sweetheart. Are you sure there's nothing else troubling you?"

"No, nothing. You know how it is during an investigation, Mum. Enjoy your evening."

"I will. You too. If you fancy a chat later, we should be home by eight."

"I'll bear it in mind. I think I'm going to fix myself an omelette and go straight to bed."

"Bless you. We did make a night of it last night. Have you heard from Nathan today?"

"No, not at all. I'll call him and then go to bed."

"Love you, daughter of mine. Maybe we can catch up tomorrow, make the most of it while we're here."

"That's it, heap the guilt on my shoulders."

"Don't be so ridiculous. I'm doing nothing of the sort. Take care. I'm going now. Tony is impatiently telling me to wind up my conversation."

Imagining the scene, Charlie laughed. "Then you'd better not keep him waiting." She ended the call and drove home, accompanied by the radio, her thoughts firmly fixed on what she'd discovered during the day. She turned the corner and let out a groan the second she saw Nathan's car parked outside her house. "Shit! I can do without this. I haven't had a chance to get my head around the information I've discovered yet."

He waved when he spotted her, and she drew her vehicle to a halt in front of his, ensuring she left enough room for him to get out. She really didn't have it in her to have company tonight. She gathered her handbag and forced a smile into place. Then she met him on the pavement outside her house. He bent down to kiss her, but she turned her face, and his lips landed on her cheek instead of her mouth.

"What are you doing here?" she asked. Her tone sounded off even to her own ears.

"I thought I'd drop by and see you. My last appointment was up the road. Is everything all right?"

She inserted the key in the front door and threw over her shoulder, "I wish people would stop asking me that."

"Sorry? What's going on here, Charlie?"

She sighed. "I'm tired. I've not been right all day. I'm going to fix myself an omelette then go to bed."

"Oh, right." He kissed the back of her neck, sending shivers running down her spine. "I could join you."

She entered the house without answering him. After they took their shoes off at the front door, he followed her through to the kitchen. He passed her and filled the kettle. Charlie struggled to look him in the eye. She sat at the small kitchen table and studied her phone.

He prepared the mugs with milk, sugar and coffee then sat opposite her. His hand crawled across the table, something he usually did. Tonight, however, the movement annoyed her. She removed her hands from the table and tucked them into her lap.

"Is there something wrong?" he asked.

"You tell me," she replied after a moment's pause.

"Charlie. I'm not a mind reader. If I've done something wrong, you need to tell me what it is, and I'll try to put it right."

She glanced up and stared at him as if seeing the real Nathan for the first time. "Who was she?"

He flung himself back in his chair. "Who? What are you bloody talking about?"

"That woman, last night. Who is she?"

"My mother? Is that who you're referring to?"

She swallowed down the acid searing her throat and watched his eyes form narrow slits. "You know damn well who I'm talking about. *Who is she?*"

"What's going on here? Why don't you believe me?"

"This is your last chance to tell me the truth." She twiddled with her engagement ring on her finger. If he didn't tell her, she'd take great pleasure in throwing it at him.

He sighed, and his gaze dropped to his hands. "What do you know?"

"Plenty. I'm waiting."

"A friend of the family. My mother isn't well at the moment."

The fact that he was avoiding eye contact with her was beginning to piss her off. "Look at me!" she shouted.

He raised his head, and she could see the terror in his eyes.

"I'm sorry. I should never have tried to deceive you. I wanted to tell you the truth. I thought it would have spoilt our evening. We had a good time, didn't we? Celebrating our engagement with your mother and Tony? There was no real harm done, Charlie, was there?"

She tucked a loose strand of hair behind her ear. "I repeat, you deceived me. What else have you lied about since we've been going out together? Because right now, I feel like there's more you're holding back from me."

"I'm not. It's the first lie I've told you. It was out of necessity."

"Necessity? Getting a stranger to pretend she's your mother? Why?"

"I wanted to impress your mother and Tony. They were expecting Mum to be there last night. She rang me during the day to tell me that she was ill and was going to bed. I had to think on my feet and thought Mum's friend could stand in for her."

"Why not simply tell the truth? Why lie and get that woman to pretend she was your mother? And while we're at it, why use a different name? Your mother is called Olivia. Surely you can understand why I'm so angry with you, can't you?"

"Yes. I admit what I did was wrong..." He ran a hand through his short hair and growled. "I don't know why I did it, other than because I'm a grade-A prick. Will you ever be able to forgive me?"

"I doubt it. I hate liars. I'm a frigging police officer, for fuck's sake." She turned away from him. "I should have known there was something wrong. I've never deserved to be happy. A man has let me down yet again."

He stared at her, the silence lingering heavily between them. Suddenly, his lip curled. "Here we go... harking on your past, as usual."

She frowned and shook her head. "I'm doing nothing of the sort. You're in the wrong here, not me. Trying to pass that woman off as your mother. Who in their right mind would do that?"

He flew out of his chair and rounded the table, grabbing her by the arms and forcing her to stand.

"Ouch. Nathan, you're hurting me."

"Am I? And what the hell do you think you're doing to me with your twisted words? One lousy mistake and you come down on me like a ton of bricks. What the fuck? Why?"

Charlie tried to shrug his hands off, but his fingers dug into her arms, causing her to wince. "You're hurting me," she repeated. "If you don't stop it, I could arrest you for assault."

He released her arms and stormed across the room to finish making the drinks. He mumbled an apology as he poured the water into the mugs.

Charlie stared at him, trying to figure out how someone could change so much at the flick of a switch. "Help me understand why you felt the need to do it."

"It was a mistake. I should have known better than to try to pull the wool over your eyes."

"So why did you?"

He stirred the drinks and then handed her a mug. He chinked the edge against hers. "To us. If there is still an *us*."

Charlie closed her eyes and leaned against the island. She opened them to find him staring at her, a hurt look emanating from his eyes.

"I don't know. You seem to be content to brush the incident off as if it doesn't matter, but the truth is that it matters a great deal to me. If you're prepared to lie or set out to deceive me about this, I can't help but wonder what else you're hiding from me. Or would be prepared to hide from me in the future. Go on, tell me I'm being unreasonable."

He took a step towards her, his arms outstretched. "I'm such an idiot. I don't know what came over me. I thought I was doing the right thing. Please forgive me, Charlie." He bent down and kissed her on the cheek.

"Maybe in time. I think it would be better if you leave. I'm exhausted and I was looking forward to having an early night."

"Without me?"

"Yes. I need you to give me some space." Charlie's phone rang. She answered it, "Hi, Mum."

He took a sip of his coffee, waved, and then walked towards the front door.

Charlie didn't have it in her to stop him. Instead, she turned her back and continued her conversation with her mother. "How's Carol doing?"

"She's feeling better. There's a chance they're going to let her out tomorrow. They're being optimistically cautious about it."

"I'll keep my fingers crossed for her."

"You sound exhausted. Have you eaten yet?"

"I am. No. I'm going to fix myself something to eat and head up to bed. It's been another frustrating day. Two women who know each other going missing is always a challenge, as you can imagine."

"I know I shouldn't say this but, if you need a hand while we're here, you only have to shout."

Charlie laughed. "Yeah, right! DCI Roberts would love that, wouldn't he?"

"Er... maybe not."

"When are you thinking about heading home?"

"We'll see how Carol settles first when they discharge her. I've already run it past Sally. She's told us to stay down here for an extra day or two, so I might do that. However, there's the kennel to consider, as well."

"Yeah, life isn't easy for you in the slightest, is it?"

"We deal with it most days. Go on, although it's lovely to catch up with you, I can hear how tired you are. I'll ring you tomorrow, let you know one way or the other if Carol gets released. Sleep well, darling."

"I'm sure I will. Give my love to Tony. Love you, Mum."

"Love you, too." Her mother blew her a kiss.

Charlie reciprocated and then hung up.

She collected the ingredients from the fridge and knocked up the omelette within minutes. While it was cooking in the pan, she switched on the grill to warm it up. There's nothing like a fluffy omelette to put the world to rights. She decided to add some chorizo to it; she'd never done that before.

Once it was ready, she carried her plate and what was left of her coffee through to the lounge to see what rubbish was on the TV, not that she was really interested. As soon as she'd eaten her dinner, she'd go to bed, anyway. It didn't feel right taking her dinner up to bed with her. She caught the tail end of the news, which stated that there had been a search in progress down by the canal, but, as yet, there was no further news from the police about the incident.

Charlie wondered if Katy should call a press conference in the morning now that there were two women missing.

Who knows where it will end if we don't get the word out?

She removed her notebook from her pocket and jotted the reminder down. She ended up flicking back through the information she had discovered about Nathan. Tears misted her vision, and she wiped them away.

I'm strong. I can deal with this. I'll see how things go between us. It's not too late to call a halt to the engagement. I need someone I can trust by my side for the rest of my life, not a man who is prepared to pass a strange woman off as his mother. I still don't understand why he did it, or his blasé attitude about the incident, as if it were just a blip in our relationship rather than something major when I had challenged him. How can I trust him again? It's going to take a while for him to regain that trust. Maybe it was too soon for us to get engaged. I obviously don't know him as well as I thought I did.

She switched off the TV and took her empty plate through to the kitchen. After rinsing it under the tap, she left it to drain overnight. Charlie checked that the front and back doors were locked and then took a glass of wine up to bed with her. She took a quick shower, careful not to wet her hair, then settled into bed with her Kindle. There was a good thriller she'd been meaning to read for a while, but everything had been full-on for months now.

Her eyelids began to droop half an hour later. She put her Kindle on the bedside table beside her and snuggled under the quilt.

Several hours later, Charlie heard a noise in her bedroom. She reached out to turn the light on, but someone struck her hand with a metal bar. "What do you want?" She thought about screaming but decided it would be pointless as most of her neighbours were elderly and probably wouldn't hear her.

"You," the automated voice said. "Get dressed. No funny business; otherwise, I will hurt you."

By the build of the intruder, she could tell it was a man. He slapped the metal bar in the palm of his hand, emphasising his point.

She flicked the quilt back, thankful she'd decided to wear her cosy pyjamas.

"Make it snappy, I haven't got all day."

"Who are you?"

He took a step towards her and raised the bar above his head. "Don't push me, bitch. I've told you what to do; now do it."

Charlie rifled through her drawers and wardrobe to find something suitable to wear for her abduction.

"Jesus! You're trying my patience now. Step aside and I'll choose an outfit for you."

He removed a pair of jeans from the wardrobe and a red jumper from one of her drawers and threw them at her, along with fresh underwear. "Put them on."

Hesitantly, she slipped off her pyjama bottoms and stepped into her panties and the jeans. She turned her back on him to complete her ensemble.

He laughed. "It's nothing I haven't seen before, love. You're nothing special. Now, get downstairs. Any funny business, and I'll clobber you. You hear me?"

"Yes."

He followed her down the stairs. Charlie's mind was racing, trying to come up with a plan to get herself out of this situation, but her brain failed her. When they reached the hallway, he was still behind her. He whacked her around the head, and she stumbled to the floor. The last thing she saw before passing out was the man towering over her, about to pull off his mask.

. . .

CHARLIE WOKE UP, maybe hours or perhaps days later, in a cell.

"She's coming around," a female voice said.

Charlie cautiously moved her head to the side. "Where am I?"

"Hello, I'm Davina, and this is Isla. We've been abducted by a man. He's been holding us in this cellar."

Charlie gingerly sat up and rested her back against the stone wall. "Shit! I'm one of the police officers who has been investigating your case." She put her hand through her hair; it was tangled and sticky with blood. "The bastard broke into my home and smacked me round the head with a metal pole. Can one of you examine the wound for me?"

Davina shuffled forward on the mattress they were sharing and turned Charlie to where there was enough light to access the wound. "It's very bloody. I can't really tell how bad it is, not in this light, I'm sorry."

"It's okay. Can you tell if it's still bleeding?"

"I don't think so."

"Thanks."

Davina returned to her place at the bottom of the bed. Charlie noticed the woman was wearing a hessian sack. She stared down and realised she was wearing the same. "Why has he removed our clothes?"

"We don't know. He's not said much to us, not since we arrived."

"Do you know him? He was wearing a mask when he broke into my house. He was about to remove it after he hit me, but I passed out before he revealed his face."

"Yes, we both went to university with him. He's called..."

"Nathan Cole," Charlie finished off for Davina.

"Yes. Oh God, does this mean you know it's him? That your team are closing in on him?" Isla asked.

Charlie sighed heavily. "I wish. I stumbled across the information yesterday, but I kept it from my colleagues."

The women both gasped.

"Why would you do that?" Davina demanded, her brow furrowed.

"I thought I was doing the right thing at the time. I was going to conduct further searches before I alerted my boss and the rest of the team."

"But why? I don't understand why you wouldn't share the information with them," Isla said.

Charlie closed her eyes and concentrated on keeping the threatening vomit from emerging. When she opened them again, both women were staring at her, waiting for an answer.

"Because... he's my fiancé!"

7

Lorne paced the floor in the lounge, annoying her husband.

"Will you sit down? The hospital will ring once the doctor has visited the ward. That might not be for hours yet, and you're already driving me crazy."

She threw herself onto the sofa beside him and kissed him on the cheek. "Sorry. I'm not sure what's up with me today. My stomach is churning, sensing that something bad is going to happen. I hope Carol doesn't have a relapse and they decide to keep her in."

"If she does, then there's nothing we can do about it. What's the point in worrying. Chill, woman, that's an order."

She snuggled into him for a cuddle. The intimate moment was disturbed a few minutes later when Lorne's mobile rang. "Hello, Lorne Warner speaking."

"Lorne, it's Katy. Sorry to disturb you. I was wondering if you'd heard from Charlie today."

Lorne sat upright. Her eyes widened as she stared at Tony.

"What is it?" he mouthed.

"I'm going to put you on speaker, Katy; Tony is here with me."

"That's fine. Have you heard from her?"

"No. She rang me last night, told me she was shattered, and said she was going to grab an early night. I take it she hasn't shown up for work this morning?"

"No. This is so unlike her. I want to go round there and see if she's okay. The thing is, I haven't got a spare key. Have you got one?"

"No. She's never got around to giving us one, no need when we live so far away."

"Would Nathan have one?"

"Probably. I'll call him. Why don't you leave this to us? As it is, you have enough on your plate at the station."

"Thanks. You're right. Okay. Let me know how you get on as soon as possible."

"Don't worry, we will."

Katy hung up, and Lorne immediately dialled Nathan's number. He answered on the second ring.

"Nathan? Hi, it's Lorne. I don't suppose you've heard from Charlie today, have you?"

"No, not at all. Is something wrong?"

"There might be. Do you have a key to her house?"

"Yes, she gave me one the other week. Do you want me to go round there and see if she's okay? Hang on, shouldn't she be at work today?"

"Yes, sorry, I should have said. Katy rang me, concerned that Charlie hadn't shown up for her shift. I said we'd drop by the house but realised I didn't have a key."

"I'm in between jobs at the moment. I can pop over there now."

"Thanks. We'll meet you there."

"I should be there in about twenty minutes."

"Okay, we'll leave shortly. Thanks for this; sorry to put you out."

"You're not, so stop fretting about that. I hope Charlie is all right."

"So do we. See you soon." She threw her phone on the cushion beside her and fell into Tony's outstretched arms. "I knew there was something wrong. I just assumed we were about to get bad news about Carol. Oh God, I dread to think what's happened to Charlie."

"There's no sense in getting yourself worked up about things, sweetheart. She probably took a sleeping pill, and it's knocked her out."

Lorne sat up and picked up her phone to dial Charlie's number. It rang until the voicemail kicked in. "Hi, Charlie, it's me. Let me know you're all right, please. Love you." She leapt off the sofa and began pacing the floor again. "Sorry if this pisses you off, but if I don't do it, I'm going to lose my mind."

Tony grinned and rose to his feet. "I have to go to the loo anyway. We'll get on the road in five minutes, so feel free to pace until then."

They kissed as he passed.

Why am I so anxious? Because that's why we're here. Carol warned us that Charlie was in danger, and now... no, I mustn't think like that. Not yet, not until we know for sure what's going on. Please, please, God, keep her safe.

Tony reappeared a few minutes later. "Are you ready? We can take a slow ride over there and have a look around before Nathan shows up."

"Excellent idea. I need to go to the loo first. I'll be two minutes."

"I'll be warming up the car."

Fifteen minutes later, they drew up outside Charlie's house, and Lorne immediately knew that something bad had happened. "Shit! The front door is open."

They tore out of the car, and Tony inspected the damage to the front door.

"Bloody hell. I reckon a crowbar has been used."

"Bugger. The same as Carol's front door. What the fuck is going on? Charlie? Are you here?"

"I'll search downstairs," Tony shouted. He ran the length of the hallway.

Lorne took the stairs two at a time. She checked the bathroom as she passed it. Nothing in there. Then she ran into the main bedroom and found Charlie's pyjamas lying on the floor and the bed unmade. *She would never leave the house without making her bed first.* She checked the en suite. There was no sign of the shower having been used, and the basin was bone-dry. Lorne lifted the pillow and found her daughter's phone. Her heart sank.

"Lorne, you'd better come down here," Tony shouted.

"On my way. There's nothing up here. I've found her phone. It was under her pillow," she said while she tore down the stairs to meet him.

He was standing in the hallway, pointing at a patch of blood on the carpet that they had missed on the way in.

Lorne's shaking hand covered her mouth, and fear clutched her heart. She reached for Tony. He threw an arm around her shoulder. "We should call Katy. She can get SOCO over here."

Lorne passed her mobile to him. "Can you do it?"

He unlocked her phone and rang Katy's number. "Hi, Katy, it's Tony. We're at Charlie's house. She's had a break-in, and there's a patch of blood on the hall carpet. Can you get SOCO here?"

"Shit! Shit! Shit! Leave it with me. I'll come over there myself. See you soon."

Tony ended the call and turned when a noise sounded behind them. It was Nathan.

"Hi, is everything okay? I didn't think you had a key. How did you get in?"

Tony pointed out the damage to the front door.

"Oops, I didn't see that. What does it mean? Where's Charlie?" He glanced down and saw the patch of blood on the carpet. "Fuck! Whose is that?"

"We're assuming it's Charlie's," Lorne said and sniffled.

Tony passed her a tissue. "We should move away from the area. Keep it as clean as possible for when SOCO arrive."

"Have you called them?" Nathan asked.

"Yes, well, I rang Katy. She's on her way over here. She's going to make arrangements for SOCO to come."

"Thank God for that. What do you think has happened?" Nathan asked, his gaze shifting between Lorne and Tony.

Lorne stared at him as if he were from another planet. "What do you think?"

"I don't know. Maybe she's had an accident or something and gone to the hospital."

Tony went to the front door. "I hadn't noticed it when we pulled up, but her car is outside."

Lorne sobbed. Clutching Charlie's phone to her heart, she walked down the hallway to the kitchen.

"We'd better leave the area clear," Tony advised Nathan.

"I don't know what to do for the best. Should I go out and look for her? What if she's injured and out there, needing help?"

"No. I think we should leave that up to Katy to organise. She'll be here soon. Let's wait in the kitchen. I'll close the door the best I can."

Nathan and Tony joined Lorne in the kitchen. She had boiled the kettle and was getting the mugs ready.

"I'll do that," Tony said. He took over the task and said, "Why don't you take a seat?"

She drifted over to the table and sat with her head buried in her hands. "Why? I can't bear the thought of her being in another vile criminal's clutches."

Nathan sat next to Lorne and put a hand on her arm. "We mustn't think the worst. She's a strong girl—resilient; she won't allow herself to be manipulated by another man, not after her last experience. What am I saying? I don't know that. The memories might come flooding back to her and..."

"Stop it! Stop it! Don't say anything else. You've only just met her. How can you possibly know what she went through?"

"Lorne, don't say that," Tony said. "He's known her long enough. Charlie's bound to have confided in him."

She plucked a tissue from the box beside her and blew her nose. "I'm sorry. I shouldn't be taking this out on you, Nathan. It doesn't matter what Charlie has told you; she never reveals the full extent of what she went through. I can't go into details, but no child—because that's what she was at the time—should ever be subjected to the torture she went through."

"I understand. Like you say, she's only told me the bare facts of what happened. But the criminal who did that to her is dead, isn't he?"

"Yes. Tony and I saw to that. We hunted him down and…"

"Lorne, that's enough. We don't have to go over old ground. Leave it in the past where it belongs."

"I'm sorry. Tony, I'm scared. She was just getting her life on track, and now this happens. Life can be so unfair."

He hugged her, and she rested her head on his chest. "I know you are. Have faith in Charlie. She's no longer an innocent child. She's got your resilience. We need to keep thinking positively."

She pulled away and glanced up at him. "If only Carol were better, she'd be able to tell us who has her."

"Would she?" Nathan asked. "Is she that good?"

"She's the best there is. Carol was instrumental in the last investigation we solved."

"Gosh, in that case, we could really do with her expertise now," Nathan said. "Any sign of her coming home yet?"

Lorne shook her head. "We're not sure. All being well, they might release her today, but she needs time to recover. She's the reason we're here."

"Lorne, don't," Tony warned.

Nathan frowned. "I don't understand."

"He has a right to know," she said.

Tony shrugged. "I wouldn't. It's your call."

"What is?" Nathan asked. "You've piqued my interest. Surely, as her fiancé, I have a right to know if you have any information about her disappearance. Please tell me."

Lorne stepped out of the embrace with Tony and rested against the worktop. She ran a hand around her face and swallowed. "Carol had a premonition that Charlie was in danger. She persuaded us to bring her home and to stay with her, just in case anything happened to our daughter."

Nathan stared at her. "Shit! Charlie didn't tell me."

Lorne wagged her finger. "Don't blame Charlie; it's my fault."

"What do you mean?" Nathan asked.

Lorne sighed. "I didn't tell her."

"What the fuck? Why not?"

"Because everything was going well for her. Your engagement, for example. I didn't see any reason to upset her."

"And by keeping quiet, all you've succeeded in doing is putting her in jeopardy. What kind of mother does that?"

"Hey, you can pack that in," Tony said angrily. "You have no idea what our daughter has been through over the years. In my opinion, Lorne did the right thing by keeping this from her."

"Obviously. I don't understand you two at all. In my opinion you've behaved abysmally. She should have been told the truth. If you believe in Carol's talents… Jesus, I can't believe what I'm hearing."

"What's going on?" Katy asked from the doorway.

Lorne flew into Katy's arms, almost knocking her over. "Oh, Katy. What are we going to do?"

"We're going to sit down and figure this out together. I get the impression I've walked in on something, have I? What's going on?"

"Yes, come on, Lorne. Tell her! Or was Katy already in on this secret?" Nathan asked. He crossed his arms and glared at her.

"Wait. What secret?" Katy demanded.

Lorne covered her eyes and sobbed.

Tony threw an arm around her shoulders. "We came down here for a reason."

"Which was?"

"Carol told us that Charlie was in trouble."

"Jesus Christ," Katy said. "What possessed you to keep that information from me?"

Lorne wiped her eyes on her sleeve. "In our defence, we thought she was safe."

"Did you mention it to Charlie?" Katy asked.

Lorne sighed and placed her head in her hands. "No. We regret that decision now. In fairness, we've been distracted by what happened to Carol. Then we had the engagement party to get ready for, you know, shopping for outfits and then going to the dinner itself.

We've barely spoken to Charlie since we arrived." Lorne's mobile rang. She rushed to remove it from her pocket in case it was Charlie. It was Sally. "I need to take this." She walked towards the back door to speak to her friend. "Hi."

"Hey, you. How's it going down there? More to the point, how is Carol doing?"

"Oh, Sally. She's gone!" Lorne struggled to hold her emotions together. She burst into tears.

Sally gasped. "What? She's dead? Oh God, I'm so sorry, Lorne."

Lorne held the phone out to Tony, who took over the call.

"Lorne, Lorne, talk to me."

"Hi, Sal. It's Tony. Lorne's too upset to speak. I'm going to put you on speaker. Katy and Nathan are here, too."

"I don't understand, Tony. Why? Is Carol dead or not?"

"No. Carol is still in hospital. We're all at Charlie's house. She's missing. We think she's been abducted. The door was open when Lorne and I got here."

"For fuck's sake! I'm coming down there—no arguments. The team can handle things at this end. I'll be with you in a couple of hours. I'm sure Simon will want to come, too."

"Thank you, Sally," Lorne whispered. "You're a true friend."

"We're more than that. You're all family, Charlie included. Try not to think negatively, Lorne. She's got your determination and strength in her genes."

"That's what I told her," Tony agreed. "We'll see you soon. We really appreciate it, Sal."

"TTFN."

Tony pressed the End Call button, placed the phone on the worktop and hugged Lorne, squeezing her so tight he cut off her air and left her gasping for breath. "Sorry, I was a bit overzealous there."

"You could say that. What are we going to do, Katy? Should we wait for Sally to arrive?"

"No. I think we should get the ball rolling ASAP. I'm going to need to inform Roberts before he hears it from someone else. Can you deal with SOCO and then follow me to the station?"

"Does that include me?" Nathan asked.

Katy was the first to respond. "Sorry, this is official police business. Members of the public aren't allowed in the station."

"That's bloody laughable. I detest the way I've been kept in the dark about this. She's my fiancée. Doesn't that count for anything? Surely, I have a right to be involved."

Lorne was seething at his outburst. In her opinion, it was uncalled for. However, as they were in Katy's territory, she allowed her former partner to inform him of his rights.

"Sorry, Nathan, this is a police matter. Lorne is her next of kin."

He threw his arm up in the air and stormed out of the room. "Screw the lot of you. I'll carry out my own search for her."

"Nathan, there's no need for you to be like this," Katy called after him. "Come back."

Lorne gripped her arm. "Let him go, Katy. I can do without the extra hassle."

"Lorne's right, Katy. He shouldn't be here. Despite being personally involved, you know that Lorne and I will both have clear heads to deal with what lies ahead of us. We barely know Nathan. We don't know what his reaction will be, although judging by what we've just witnessed, it wouldn't take much to work out."

Katy nodded. "I agree. Shit, I could do with you two coming back to the station with me to get the investigation underway."

"Why doesn't Lorne go with you? I'll hang around here and wait for the tech guys to show up and do the necessary. I could have a go at repairing the door myself and join you at the station later."

"There's no need. I'll instruct the handyman to come out again. But yes, if you can oversee all of that for us, it will enable us to crack on."

"Go for it." He hugged Lorne and kissed the top of her head. "You're in safe hands with Katy and the team, and Sally is on her way, too. Promise me that you will stay calm and positive at all times."

Lorne smiled up at him. "I'll try my best. Join us as soon as you can."

"Yes, the same rules don't apply to you, Tony, as they do to Nathan. I'll make sure everyone is aware of that back at the station."

"Thanks, Katy. Good luck with convincing Roberts. He might need some persuading to the contrary."

"Leave him to me. We'll head off now. I'll call the handyman en route."

Lorne and Katy left the property and jumped into Katy's car. "How are you holding up?" Katy asked as they set off.

"Barely would be my response. All the bad memories have flooded back. Charlie doesn't deserve this. Why her? Does she attract weirdos, or what?"

"We'll get to the bottom of it, Lorne, you have my word. I think it's safe to assume that there must be a connection with the other two missing women. It's too much of a coincidence otherwise."

"How far have you got with the investigation?"

"Not far at all. We're searching the girls' SM accounts to see if anything else stands out for us to investigate. As it stands, all we've found is that they attended Oxford together."

"Ah, yes. It came up over dinner the other night that Nathan knew the first girl, Davina. He mentioned it while we were eating. Actually, Nathan's mother was interested in what sort of investigation Charlie was working on at the time."

"Gotcha. The other woman, Isla, wasn't reported missing until yesterday. Now Charlie is gone, as well, and I'm struggling to see how. It's not like she has been investigating the case alone. She's been by my side every time we've left the station."

"Maybe someone you've questioned over the past couple of days has had their eye on Charlie; perhaps they followed her home."

"It seems the most likely scenario. Maybe we should revisit those people as a priority, not that we've interviewed that many people on this one, yet."

Lorne tutted. "Perhaps someone has been watching her for months and has decided to make their move now, knowing that we would make the connection with the ongoing investigation."

"Possibly. It's worth considering, Lorne. Jesus, I hope she's safe."

"Don't! I can't bear to think of her being in danger again. She suffered so much at the hands of that bastard."

"I'm sure she'll be fine. Please believe in her. She's come on leaps and bounds over the past year and has grown considerably in confidence since achieving her promotion."

"Let's hope you're right. We both know there are hordes of depraved individuals walking the streets of London. To target a copper is pushing the boundaries but not inconceivable, especially if they intend using her as a bargaining tool." Katy slammed the heel of her hand onto the steering wheel. "Yes, I bet that's what we're up against here. Someone has a relative or friend on the inside and their intention is to barter their freedom for Charlie's."

Lorne shook her head. "I can't see it. However, it would be foolish of us to dismiss the idea at this stage with very little evidence to go on."

The rest of the journey was carried out in silence, both deep in thought. Katy pulled into her parking space, and Lorne sucked in a deep breath as she stepped out of the vehicle.

"Are you nervous at being back?"

"I think so. My stomach is tied up in knots because Charlie is missing; I could do without having to meet Roberts again and, of course, this place holds so many memories for me—not all of them good."

Katy hooked an arm through hers. "You'll be fine. The team will welcome you. I'm not sure how Roberts is going to react, yet. We'll soon find out. I'll get you settled with the team and then I'll visit Roberts. I'd better do that first thing. That bloke has a sixth sense when something isn't right and tends to pop up when you least expect him to. I'd rather bite the bullet early than get found out and have him make a fool of me in front of the others."

"I hear you. What you're really telling me is that he's still as unpredictable as ever, right?"

They both grinned.

"You've got it. Keep smiling, Lorne, it'll help to get you through this. We're both churning up inside. The unknown has a habit of doing that to you."

The desk sergeant was made aware of the situation and signed Lorne in on the guest register. "It's good to have you back, even under these dreadful circumstances, ma'am."

"Thanks, Sergeant." Lorne didn't have it in her to get into a conversation with him about his family; she was eager to get on.

They entered the security door and climbed the stairs, still deep in conversation—so much so that they neglected to see DCI Sean Roberts standing at the top of the stairs, waiting for them.

"Well, look who it is. Lorne Simpkins."

"Warner," Lorne corrected him. She swallowed down the bile that rose in her throat and fixed a smile in place.

"Ah, yes. How remiss of me to forget that. To what do we owe the pleasure?" His gaze ran the length of her body.

Lorne felt awkward, but Katy had advised her to leave the explaining for her to do.

"Why don't we discuss this in your office, sir?" Katy suggested.

He folded his arms and tapped his foot on the concrete floor. "I think here will do nicely. I'm waiting."

Katy shrugged. "Very well. Charlie has gone missing."

He frowned and uncrossed his arms. "She what? Tell me more."

Several officers passed them in the hallway.

"I'd rather do this in private, sir, for obvious reasons."

"Yes, of course. Your office is nearer. I want to hear all the facts from you, Katy, no one else."

Lorne's heart sank. He hadn't changed one bit. He'd always had it in for her since the day he'd taken up his position. He'd made her life hell, and it had been an absolute privilege to hand in her resignation when the time had come. She was shocked when Charlie had told her that she got on well with Roberts.

KATY AND ROBERTS relocated to her office, where she brought him up to date on what had been going on.

"Why kidnap Charlie?" he asked.

"With respect, sir, if I knew that, I wouldn't be sitting here right now; I'd be out there hunting the bastard down."

"All right, Katy, there's no need to talk to me in that tone."

"I'm sorry. Lorne and I are both really concerned about what might happen to Charlie and how she's going to react, given what's taken place in her past."

"I understand and fully appreciate your concerns, but from what I've seen, Charlie has her mother's defiant genes running through her. They might not have surfaced as yet, but I can tell they're bubbling under the surface. She'll be on her guard at all times."

Katy muttered something she never thought she would ever say about her partner: "If she's still alive."

"Shit! Don't let her mother hear you say that. She'd slit your throat for even thinking it."

"Bollocks. Sorry for swearing, but why have you always had such a downer on Lorne? She's one of the best officers this station—and the Met itself—has ever had, and yet, even now, when her daughter's life is at risk, you're sitting here taking pot shots at her."

"I dispute that. You must admit, I have never let my fraught relationship with her mother interfere with how I get along with Charlie. Lorne and I have a lot of history under our belts. She has proven to be a wildcard over the years and tried my patience on many occasions. You and I have never had an issue, have we?"

Katy shook her head. "No, never."

"I rest my case. Lorne and I rubbed each other up the wrong way. That said, I'm willing to set aside any personal issues I might have with the woman until Charlie has been found, who I regard as an exceptional member of this team."

"I agree. We owe it to Charlie to give this investigation everything we've got... umm... that includes working alongside Lorne and her husband, Tony."

Roberts rolled his eyes. "He's here, as well?"

"He's overseeing the repairs and SOCO techs at Charlie's house."

"Are you telling me she was abducted from her home?"

"Yes. It would seem during the night. Lorne spoke to her not long after she finished work yesterday. Charlie told her she was exhausted and was looking forward to having an early night. She wasn't at her best yesterday."

"Oh, in what way?"

"Upon reflection, she seemed distracted all day. The previous evening, she went out for a celebratory dinner with Lorne, Tony and Nathan."

His eyes narrowed. "Who is this Nathan?"

"Her fiancé. They just got engaged."

"Shit! It's news to me that she was seeing anyone, let alone that she had got engaged to him. And where is this fiancé of hers?"

"I went to the house to see the damage for myself. He was there. He offered to help search for Charlie. I had to let him down lightly, telling him that this is a police investigation and that Lorne is Charlie's next of kin."

"Ouch! I bet that went down like a lead balloon."

"I admit, I could have handled it better. He stormed out of the house, flinging over his shoulder the fact that he was going to search for Charlie himself."

"Silly man. I hope for your sake he doesn't get in the way."

Katy held up her crossed fingers. "Me too. I suppose he had a right to be angry. I would feel the same way if I were in his shoes. It's obvious how much he loves Charlie."

"While I have every sympathy with the young man, in these circumstances he should leave the investigation to the professionals. Apparently, we're inundated with them at the moment."

"There's something else I haven't told you."

He groaned. "I'm sensing I'm not going to like what you have to say, am I?"

"Possibly. Lorne has been in touch with her boss and partner, DI Sally Parker, and she's on her way down here to lend a hand."

"Jesus! Lend a hand or take over the investigation?"

"I won't let that happen. Lorne, Sally and Tony will all be told that everything they uncover has to go through me. They won't be allowed to make any move under their own steam."

He cocked an eyebrow and chortled. "Good luck with that one. This is Lorne Simpkins, sorry, I'll correct that, Warner, we're talking about here."

Katy smiled. "I know. She'll behave; otherwise, I will ban her from the station, no doubt with your backing."

"Definitely. Is there anything else I should know?"

Katy ran through the facts they had learnt regarding the two other women who had been reported missing.

"You believe Charlie has been abducted by the same person who has these two women?"

"Maybe. Until we discover any evidence that tells us otherwise."

"I think you should proceed with caution. Don't limit your investigation."

"We won't, don't worry."

He rose from his seat and opened the door. "You know where I am if you need any extra advice. That's not to say you're not capable of running an investigation of this magnitude. I believe in you. Bring Charlie home safely, Katy."

She followed him out of the office and watched as he passed Lorne and whispered something in her ear.

Katy was dying to find out what he'd said. She rushed over to Lorne, expecting her to be upset by his words. Instead, she was smiling and had tears in her eyes.

"Blimey, what did he say to spark that kind of reaction in you?"

"He apologised for being a grouch and wished us luck in getting Charlie back. I think I need to sit down." Lorne stumbled backwards into a spare chair.

Katy laughed. "Bloody hell, I never expected him to say that, not after the reception he gave you outside."

"He's an unknown quantity at the best of times. He never ceases to amaze me. I'll be wary, though. He's pulled the rug from under my feet more times than I care to mention over the years."

8

The door to the cellar opened, and the other two women gasped and clung to each other. Charlie watched Nathan descend the stairs, nothing but hatred searing her veins. As he came into view, his gaze locked on to hers, and he grinned at her.

He approached the bars and clung to them. "Hello, my love. How are you and your new playmates doing?"

Charlie glared at him and said one word: "Why?"

He tutted and narrowed his eyes. "Now then, Charlie, if I let all of my secrets out of the bag where would be the fun in that?"

"You've deceived me from the beginning, haven't you?"

His grin broadened, showing off his gleaming white teeth that he'd spent a fortune on over the years. "I might have. It's all part of the major plan I have up my sleeve. Tell me, ladies, are you hungry?"

"Yes," Isla and Davina both said.

Charlie refused, because in all honesty, she felt sick to her stomach.

"Charlie?"

"No. I'd rather starve than take any food you have to offer."

"At least I'll know for the future. It makes no odds to me if you starve yourself to death or not. Mind you, you could do with shifting a few extra pounds from those legs and that backside of yours... just saying." He laughed and walked away.

Isla squeezed her shoulder. "Don't listen to him. You're fine just the way you are."

"I know his comment was below the belt and intended to destroy my confidence, but it hasn't. Don't worry about me. I think we have a long road ahead of us, ladies."

The door slammed once Nathan had reached the top of the stairs. They hugged each other, the relief evident.

Moments later, the door opened again. Nathan's footsteps echoed around the cellar. He appeared with a tray and placed it on the floor next to the cell door.

"Help yourselves, Isla and Davina. You heard what Charlie said: she'd rather starve than take any food I have to offer her. If I find out that either of you has given her some of yours... well, I'm sure you're capable of filling in the blanks." He tipped his head back and laughed. When he'd finished, his gaze searched out Charlie's again. "My, my, little one, to witness such hatred in your eyes pierces my heart. And to think, you and I only celebrated our engagement the other evening, and now, here you are, about to be..." He smirked and wagged his finger, then he tapped the side of his nose. "Another secret that I'm not yet ready to reveal."

Charlie's eyes formed tiny slits as the hatred surged. After a few moments, she smiled and cocked an eyebrow. "Bring it on. I love a good challenge; you know that as well as I do, Nathan, if that's your real name."

"It is, although Cole might not be." He wiggled his eyebrows. "There, that's a snippet of news you never expected to hear, isn't it?"

Charlie shrugged. "Nothing you say should surprise me. I don't know you at all, Nathan." Using his name made her retch.

He laughed as she gagged. "You amuse me, Charlie. All the intimate times we've spent together over the last couple of months and here you are, retching, as you release my name from those luscious lips of yours." He leaned closer to the bars and said, "By the way, all those intimate times I just referred to, nine times out of ten, I had to rush to the bathroom afterwards and vomit."

"Really?" Charlie said, not in the least bit surprised that he would predictably have a vile retort on the tip of his tongue.

"Really. Touching you was like running my hand over sandpaper. Your skin is so coarse. A bit like you: rough and ready. Yes, I used you. There, the truth has been set free." He closed his eyes and smugly said, "It's so liberating to hear that out loud."

Charlie stared at him, refusing to rise to the bait.

"Well, I must go now, ladies. Don't forget to be selfish with your food. I have eyes everywhere."

As soon as his back was turned, Charlie checked the walls and the ceiling for any type of camera he might have installed to keep an eye on them. She couldn't see any, not from where she was standing. Isla and Davina pushed past her to get to their food. They opened the foil parcel to find half a ham sandwich each.

"Is that it?" Isla asked, clearly shocked by the discovery.

"Stingy little shit," Davina said. "He was always a weirdo at uni."

The three of them sat on the only bed. Charlie deliberately kept her eyes averted, not wanting to be tempted by the sandwich Isla and Davina were sharing.

"Can you tell me what he was like at university? Is that where you met him?"

Davina finished her mouthful and was the first to speak. "I used to go out with him. It was in our first year. He turned out to be like a Jekyll and Hyde character. When we were around our friends, he would hug me close and was always whispering sweet things in my ear, but when we were alone..." She shuddered. "He was always putting me down. Criticising the way I spoke and acted. He would call me a worthless slag—sometimes even worse than that."

"That's dreadful. How did you get away from him?"

Davina placed a finger on her chin as she thought. "Now you're asking. I think I set out to make him hate me. You know, act dumb, even though I was one of the top girls in most of my classes. Eventually, he got bored with me and moved on to another girl. She was giggly and fawned all over him. I was totally fine with his decision to set me free. In fact, it made my year."

"I'm glad you escaped his clutches," Charlie said.

"I wouldn't say that," Davina replied. "Look around you."

Charlie nodded. "Yes, we'll come to that in a moment. What about you, Isla?"

"I met up with him in the second year. He went out with a friend of mine but always told me he had the hots for me. I refused to go out with him for months. In the end, he wore me down. I had the same experience as Davina. He started off charming, especially in front of others, but as soon as we were alone, it was as though he didn't know how to behave properly with a woman."

Charlie thought over her time with Nathan. Her experience had been different to theirs. Maybe he'd upped his game on purpose, and this was the end result.

"And you?" Isla asked.

Charlie shrugged. "No, he was the same with me, whether we had company or not."

"Why do you think he's abducted us? More to the point, what do you think he's going to do with us?" Davina asked.

"It would be wrong of us to speculate, but what we need to consider is that there are three of us. If we remain strong, we can overpower him. Fight for one another. He can't keep us here forever. I suspect we'll be moved, possibly in the near future. We just need to keep alert and wait for the right time to come along."

The two women glanced at each other. Charlie could see the fear settle in their eyes.

"I'm not sure if I want to risk getting him angry," Davina said.

"I agree. I suppose it'll be a case of watching and waiting to see if an opportunity arises and how we feel about tackling him when the time comes."

Charlie shrugged and walked over to the bars. *I won't be able to do this alone. They're going to need to assist me. I'll have to work on them.* Disappointed, she turned to see both women tucking into their sandwiches. Even if she was hungry, she knew her stomach would reject any type of food. She returned to the bed and sat at the end.

"Are you sure you don't want a nibble?" Isla offered what was left of her sandwich.

Charlie shook her head. "No, thanks. You enjoy it."

THIRTY MINUTES LATER, both women complained that they were tired and that their heads were fuzzy. Not long after, Isla and Davina passed out.

Charlie checked their pulses; they appeared to be racing. "The bastard has drugged them. Why?"

The door to the cellar opened. Not knowing what else to do, Charlie draped herself over Isla, pretending that she had been drugged, as well. She forced herself not to react when she heard two men's voices.

Nathan has brought someone to see them. Why?

"What is this, Nathan? They're all asleep."

"I might have slipped something in their food. I told the one on top not to eat anything, though. I'm disappointed in her."

"You know what women are like when there is food around," the man jested.

They both laughed. Charlie resisted the temptation to shudder, aware that the slightest movement would give the game away.

"Tell me, Nathan, what are their situations? Are they single, married, or what?"

"One is separated from her husband. Another girl is off men at the moment, and the third is... engaged to me."

"What? Why would you do this to your own fiancée?"

"It seemed a good idea at the time." Nathan laughed. "No, she's pissed me off recently, been asking too many questions, so I thought I would punish her. She's been a pain in the arse, and I want rid of her. So? Have we got a deal?"

"I'm not sure. From here, I can't see what their figures are like. They're no good to me if they are carrying extra pounds. My customers expect me to provide the best. They appreciate slender girls with curves in all the right places."

"Believe me, all three of them have curves in the right places. I've seen them all naked."

"You've been a busy boy. Okay, you've convinced me. How much do you want for them?"

"What do you think is a fair price? I'm not a greedy man," Nathan asked.

"Unlike your father, eh? I seem to remember him being a tough man to negotiate with back in the day."

Charlie's interest piqued. *His father?*

"I'll give you five million for all three of them. How's that?"

"Sounds good to me."

"I will get my boys to come and pick them up later. We'll make the arrangements upstairs. This place is giving me the creeps."

"It serves a purpose," Nathan said, and they both left the cellar.

As soon as she thought the coast was clear, Charlie sat upright and tried to wake Davina and Isla, but there was no response from either of them.

She suddenly felt all alone, and for the first time in over twenty years, fear emerged within her and refused to leave.

9

Sally arrived without her husband and joined the rest of the team. Lorne made her a coffee after her long trip, while Katy brought her up to date on the investigation.

"Have you begun questioning the people you've already interviewed?"

Katy sighed. "Not yet. We will do soon. You think it's one of them?"

"It seems the most obvious place to start. We won't know for sure until we've spoken to them."

"We'll split the team up. The job will be completed quicker that way," Katy agreed.

"Makes sense," Sally said. "Why do you think the perpetrator has abducted Charlie, though? Was she working on something separately from the rest of you?"

"No. Not as far as I know," Katy replied. She walked across the room to Charlie's desk and started up her computer. She paused to contemplate what Charlie's password might be. After several wrong attempts, she finally hit the right one. "Let's take a look at her browser history. She told me that Nathan went to university with the first woman who went missing, Davina Sedge. Yes, here's the proof of that. And here's Nathan in the next search. And another photo of him with his mother, Olivia."

"Wait! What did you say?" Tony shot across the room and peered over Katy's shoulder.

"What's going on?" Lorne said.

Tony pointed at the screen. "That's not the woman we met at dinner the other night."

"What the...? No, it's not. She was called Gillian. I caught her crying in the toilet. She wouldn't tell me why. None of this is making any sense."

"What did you say Nathan's surname is?" Katy asked.

"I can't remember, can you, Tony?" Lorne asked.

Tony seemed as perplexed as she was.

"I thought she said it was Cole. But don't quote me on that. Why?"

Katy glanced back at the screen and ran her finger over it as she read. "This article is calling his mother Olivia Baldwin."

Lorne's knees buckled beneath her, and Tony had to reach out to break her fall. "No, no, no. This can't be happening."

"Shit, it's not who I think it is, is it, Lorne?" Sally asked.

She tried to hold back the tears, but they refused to be suppressed. Tony guided her to the nearest chair.

Her hands trembled as she wiped away the tears. "Could it be his son?"

"Who?" Katy asked, bewildered.

"The Unicorn," Tony filled in for her.

"Oh, shit!" Katy said, shaking her head.

The whole room fell silent for a few moments.

Then Lorne asked, "Charlie didn't mention this to anyone here?"

"Not to me," Katy replied. "All this is news to me. She wasn't herself yesterday, but she told me she'd drunk too much at the dinner party. I should have pushed her. This is all my fault."

"Don't be silly," Sally intervened. "It's no one's fault. What if she confronted him about it?"

"She seemed fine when I spoke to her last night," Lorne said. "She didn't mention that she was seeing Nathan. She told me she was going to grab an early night. We need to call him."

"And say what?" Tony asked. "No, we need to play this cautiously. Maybe she tackled him, wanting to know the truth about his mother, and he got scared and decided to abduct her."

Lorne's mobile rang. "It's the hospital. I need to take it." She answered the call. "Hello, yes, that's right. Is Carol okay...? Thank you, that's wonderful news. I'll come and collect her." She sighed and hung up. "Carol has been discharged."

"I'll pick her up," Tony offered. "You stay here and try to figure this out with Sally and Katy."

Lorne left her seat to hug him. "What would I do without you?"

"Let's hope you never have to find out. I'll drop Carol home. Should I tell her what's going on?"

"See how well she is first. If she knows that Charlie is missing, she'll want to be here with us."

"I'll play it by ear. Don't do anything rash while I'm away. Promise me."

Lorne nodded. "You have my word."

"I won't be long." He kissed her and raced out of the incident room.

Lorne returned to her seat and rested her head on her arms on the desk.

Sally stood beside her and rubbed her back. "We'll find her, Lorne. Charlie's smarter than she was the last time. She'll keep her wits about her."

Lorne sat up and smiled at Sally. "I hope you're right. I can't bear the thought of losing her. Of her being in the hands of that man's son. No wonder he was asking about our trip to France."

"He was? When?" Katy asked.

"The first time we met him. He'd said he had heard all about us and... oh, it doesn't matter. It sounds like his objective was to prise information out of us, possibly to use against us. This is retribution for us killing his father."

"He must have been pumping Charlie for information from the outset. You told me the engagement came as a shock to Charlie. Maybe it was his way of trying to put her off the scent. To earn her trust quicker," Sally said. "Oh God, Lorne, I'm so sorry Charlie has found herself in this predicament. We need to keep the faith, though. Think of the positives and brush over the negatives."

Lorne puffed out her cheeks. "I'm trying. Charlie's not as strong as we all think she is. She has her vulnerable side, and I'm sure it won't take him long to figure that out."

"Her vulnerable side is her family. If he *really* wanted to hurt her, he would have come after you or Tony—but he didn't," Sally pointed out, something Lorne hadn't thought about.

Lorne clicked her fingers. "Carol! He went after her. Took her out of the equation because of her psychic abilities. Charlie has probably told him how well she did on our last case up in Norfolk, and he thought taking her out of the picture would be an advantage to him."

"It's a possibility," Katy admitted. "Charlie kept all of us informed about that case, so it's likely she told Nathan, as well."

"There's more," Lorne said. "Thinking about it properly for the first time, Charlie's door had the same sort of damage that Carol's front door sustained. The damage at Carol's suggested a crowbar had been used; SOCO noted the telltale signs of forced entry—bent metal and broken wood. For all we know, he could have one in the boot of his car or under his driver's seat. I feel pig-sick that he duped us into thinking he was something he isn't. He has his father's genes in that respect. Jesus, the connotations of all this are freaking me out. If his aim is to seek revenge, I'm not sure if we're ever going to find her. If he's as powerful as his father…"

"It sounds like you're giving up on her, Lorne," Katy said. "I refuse to do that. I'm going to have to let Roberts know what's going on."

"I'm here," he said from the doorway. "What have you found out?"

Lorne left her chair and flew into his arms, surprising not only Sean but everyone else in the room, too. "Oh, Sean. It's him."

"Katy?" he queried.

"We think we know who might have taken Charlie."

"Who?" He hugged Lorne awkwardly.

"We've worked out that Nathan, Charlie's fiancé, is none other than Robert Baldwin's son."

"The name rings a bell... oh, no, wait just a minute. The Unicorn, am I right?" He hugged Lorne properly, and she cried against his chest.

"Oh, Sean. What are we going to do? This is payback for what we did to his father."

"How sure are you?" he asked, his anger rising.

Katy ran through the evidence they had uncovered.

He shook his head and then pushed Lorne away from him. "Don't worry, we'll find her."

"I hope so. If Nathan has the same contacts open to him that his father had at his disposal, she could be shipped out of the country before we've had time to get a plan into action."

"It won't come to that," Sean assured her and hugged her to him again.

Lorne glanced up at him. "How do you know? The criminal underworld is rife in London. If he's taken over his father's role... I can't bear to think of the possibilities that will be open to him, not with Charlie's life in danger." She pulled away from her former boss and returned to her seat.

"I can have a word with a colleague of mine. He has a few underworld contacts. I'll see what I can find out and get back to you." Sean marched out of the room, a man on a mission.

Lorne placed her head in her hands. "I can't believe this is happening again... and after all these years. I thought we were all safe. I had no idea Baldwin was even married, let alone that he had a child. Nathan must have inherited his father's wicked genes. No, I can't think about that."

"No, you're right, Lorne, you need to stop speculating. We're going to have to deal with hard evidence if we're going to get her back. I think the first thing we need to do is trace Nathan's vehicle. Do you know where he lives?"

Lorne chewed her lip, then said, "No, I don't. His vehicle should be easy to trace, though. That's a good call."

"Graham, can you do that for me? Let's get cracking, team, you know what to do. Nathan is our prime suspect. Let's see what we can dig up about him. Don't forget, he's been going under the name of Cole."

"I've already started," Karen said. "He left Oxford without graduating. He's been recognised in the world of business for the past five years as one of the country's best young entrepreneurs."

"Probably using the money from his father's ill-gotten gains to fund his businesses," Lorne said bitterly.

"Wouldn't those have gone back to the government?" Katy asked.

"We're talking about the lowest of the low when it comes to criminals here, with a network that ran the length and breadth of the country. Where there's a will... He must have had funds hidden somewhere—cash that the police didn't know about. How else would Nathan have been able to start up in business?"

"Sorry, yes. You're probably right," Katy said.

"If only Charlie had told us she was seeing someone," Lorne complained.

"What use would that have been? She's had other boyfriends; your suspicions weren't raised then, were they?" Sally asked.

"No, you're right. I'm being silly. The fear growing inside me isn't allowing me to think rationally. Thinking about it, when he proposed to Charlie, she was more than taken aback when he got down on one knee in front of her."

"It was too soon; the alarm bells should have sounded in Charlie —maybe they had. Perhaps that's why she was doing the extra research on him," Katy suggested.

"More than likely. He should have kept quiet about knowing the girl who was missing, unless that was intentional on his part," Lorne said. "Either way, he's played us. Who knows where this is going to end?"

"You mustn't think like that, Lorne. There are enough professionals in this room to give you the confidence you need to see this through to the end," Sally jumped in to add.

Lorne reached for her hand. "I'm so glad you're here, keeping me on the straight and narrow."

"That's my job." Sally smiled.

WITH EVERY MEMBER of the team doing their best to find some crucial evidence against Nathan, the next twenty minutes flew by. Tony entered the room with Carol in tow. Lorne immediately told them that they had worked out who Nathan was.

Carol rushed over to where Lorne was sitting, tears running down her cheeks. "I'm sorry, love. I've let you down."

"How do you work that one out? You haven't, Carol. You were ill, recuperating in hospital. This has nothing to do with you."

"It has. If I hadn't had that migraine, I wouldn't have received the bump to the head."

"Did you see who knocked you out? If I showed you a photo, would you recognise him?" Lorne asked.

"Maybe. My head is still slightly fuzzy."

Katy drew Carol's attention. "Here he is, Carol."

Carol walked over to the screen and peered at it. "Oh, yes, that's him."

"Shit. That's Charlie's fiancé. We believe he got to you and took you out of the game after hearing about your success in the investigation up in Norfolk."

"Oh my. And he's the one who has abducted Charlie?"

"Yes. If there is anything you can do to help, now would be an excellent time, Carol."

She sat in the vacant chair behind her and rubbed her head. "I can try. Will someone make me a cup of tea?"

Katy winced. "We don't have any; we all drink coffee around here."

"I've got some in my office," Sean said, sneaking up on them again.

"I'll nip and get it," Graham said.

"What have you managed to find out, Sean?"

"I haven't, as yet. The word is out on the street. We're waiting for their response. It's good to see you again, Carol. I hear you had a lot of success up in Norfolk."

"Yes, that's right." Carol's reply was terse, to say the least. But then, she had always detested the way Sean Roberts had treated Lorne when she worked under him at the station. "I've been ill, so feeling out of sorts for a few days. It was Nathan who broke into my house and battered me."

"I'm sorry to hear that, Carol. It would appear to have been part of his plan to abduct Charlie," Tony agreed. "If you can offer any help going forward, that would be a bonus for us."

"I'm going to do my best. Hush now, I need peace and quiet."

The room fell silent. Carol went into a trance-like state. She rubbed at her temples. Lorne was tempted to ask her if she was all right, but she didn't want to disturb her in case she was in touch with the spirit world.

"Will you watch over her for us, Pete? Good man. I knew I could rely on you. Yes, I'll let them know. If there is anything around that will lead us to the location, please tell me as soon as possible... Oh, no, that's not good. Stay with her. Comfort her, if you can." Carol's head tipped back, and she exhaled the largest of breaths. "She's safe—for now. Pete's with her. He'll make sure she doesn't come to any harm."

"Thank God for that," Lorne said. "Could you see where she was?"

"Charlie is with two other women. They're being kept in some kind of cell. Pete believes it is in a cellar. I need to take a break before I try again. My head still isn't good, but it's getting better. I'm going to do my best not to let you down."

Lorne hugged her. "Thank you, Carol. Just knowing that she's still alive is a relief." She reached for Tony's hand.

He came closer and smiled.

"We'll find her," he whispered.

I hope so. I can't lose her, not to that vile man's son. When will this nightmare end?

Carol made a guttural noise and stared at the wall behind Lorne. "I'm picking up some kind of manor house. Do you know what Nathan's place looks like?"

"We haven't got an address for him yet. The team are trying to locate that information," Lorne replied. "Are there any landmarks, any other clues that we can use to identify the location, Carol?"

"There's a marbled hallway and a grand sweeping staircase over to the right. I'm not getting any warmth from the building. That could mean that either the house is empty or that it's haunted. I'm not sure which right now."

Tony clenched Lorne's hand to gain her attention. He mouthed something, but she didn't quite catch what he was saying.

"If you have something to say, Tony, let's hear it," Sean said.

"I didn't want to interrupt Carol's flow," Tony stated.

"It's fine, Tony. I'm just searching the area for clues," Carol assured him. "Have I given you something that you recognise?"

"I think so. The house we visited with Nathan the other day. It was a manor house with a marbled hallway."

"Oh heck, yes, and it had a cellar, too, didn't it?" Lorne replied. She leapt out of her seat. "He was hoping to purchase the property to renovate it and wanted our advice on whether he should buy it or not. Sick shit. Oh Christ, don't tell me the other women were there in that damn cellar while he was showing it off to us."

"Probably. What a devious fucker! Can you remember where it was?" Katy asked.

"I think so. He was driving—you know what it's like when you're a passenger—but I've got a rough idea," Tony said.

"Between us, I think we can figure out the route," Lorne confirmed.

"Okay. Let me get the team organised. I'm going to ask an Armed Response Team to accompany us," Katy said. She ran a hand through her hair.

"Let me do that for you," Sean jumped in. "It'll be better coming from me, especially when the commanding officer hears that we can't give him an address."

"Tell them it's important and that one of our officers has been abducted," Katy ordered.

Sean raised an eyebrow. "I'm aware of what I should tell them, Inspector. If they're free, I'll ask them to meet us here in fifteen minutes, if not sooner, how about that?"

"Perfect. Thank you, boss."

He rushed over to a spare desk to make the call while Katy gathered the rest of the team, including Carol.

She leaned in, keeping her voice low. "We've got this, peeps. Karen, you should stay here, and no, that's not just because you're a woman. You're the best computer whiz we've got. You can keep your eye on every aspect of the operation for us."

"No problem, boss."

"As for the rest of us, we should head off in two—no, make that three—cars, in case we have to split up and chase after him or them. At this time, we have no idea what we're up against. For all we know, he could have an army of villains at his disposal."

"Let's face it," Lorne said, "he's intentionally kept us in the dark on purpose. How did I let him fool me?"

Carol placed a hand on Lorne's arm. "It's not your fault. He's a manipulator. He had a plan and carried it out with precision. If I might make a suggestion... I don't want to step on anyone's toes here."

"Any suggestions are greatly appreciated in my team, Carol." Katy smiled. "What's on your mind?"

"Maybe you should consider sending someone to his mother's house," Carol said.

"That's a good call," Lorne replied.

"It is. I'm not sure I want to get her involved at this point, but we can certainly send a surveillance team out there. Well done, Carol. I'll see if the desk sergeant can send a patrol out there in an unmarked car, just to keep an eye on the place."

"I'm not saying she's involved," Carol added, "but there's no telling whether he'll turn up there if he knows or senses that we're on to him."

"I agree. Let me get that organised. Karen, can you give me the mother's address?"

"It's on my desk." Karen collected her notebook and handed it to Katy.

"Thanks. I'll make the call in my office. Be ready to leave in ten minutes, folks." Katy tore into her office and emerged a few minutes later. "That's all taken care of. How did you get on, sir?"

Sean nodded. "All set up. They should be with us shortly. We should work out who is going with whom. I don't mind taking my car. Why don't you come with me, Sally? Maybe Carol should tag along with you, Katy, as well as Lorne and Tony. The rest of the team can follow us."

"Sounds good to me. Does anyone have any objection to that?"

Everyone nodded their agreement.

Stephen was the closest to the window. He announced, "The ART is here."

"Okay," Katy said. "We're ready to go then. Good luck! Stay in touch if we get separated. We'll pick up the Tasers on the way out."

As it was, Tony and Lorne figured out the location using an online map.

"This is it," Lorne shouted, relieved. "I can't believe we found it."

Tony kissed her on the cheek. "I never had a doubt. Well done."

"Let's forget about congratulating ourselves until we've found Charlie and the other women," Katy warned.

They parked fifty feet from the house and congregated at the end of the street. Katy and Sean met up with the ART commanding officer. It was decided that he should take over the operation, at least until his men had gained access to the property and made it safe.

Lorne held hands with Tony on one side of her and Carol on the other.

"I'm eager to get in there," Tony said.

"You're going to have to bide your time, love."

Carol shook her head. "Something isn't right."

"What do you mean?" Katy asked, standing right behind them.

"I can't explain." Carol's head rose. She glanced up at the sky and asked, "What's going on, Pete? Oh, no. That can't be right... sorry, I wasn't doubting you."

"What did he say?" Lorne whispered.

"I got the feeling that the women are no longer here, and Pete has just backed it up."

"Shit!" Sean said. "Let's give the ART a chance to see if that's true or not before we decide what to do next."

The ART commanding officer shouted for those inside the property to show themselves. When there was no movement inside the house, his men broke down the door. The rest of the team had an anxious wait for the next few minutes until the ART reappeared. Lorne, Katy and Sean all ran towards the commanding officer, seeking news.

He ran a hand through his hair. "We found evidence in the cellar that people had been held captive. Unfortunately, it was empty. We're too late."

Lorne turned her back on the man and smashed her clenched fists against her thighs. "No, this can't be happening. So near and yet so far."

"I'm sorry, Lorne. We did our best; don't lose hope," Katy said.

Tony hugged Lorne and scanned the area. "What about the other properties? These houses must cost a fortune. Wouldn't they have cameras?"

"Hey, what's going on here? I have a right to know." A man raced towards them, a barking German shepherd by his side.

Katy showed her warrant card and approached the man. "Hello, sir. This is a police operation. I'm going to have to ask you to keep back and allow us to get on with our work."

"Oh, I see. Well, people have been coming and going all day at that house. I know it's for sale, but I'm not aware of it being sold yet. Now you lot turn up on our doorsteps. This is a quiet neighbourhood; we don't like trouble. Are you going to tell me what's going on here? I have a right to know if my property value is going to be affected by what I've seen today."

Katy's interest piqued. "Can we go back to your place and have a chat?"

"Have you got any cameras at your property, sir?" Tony shouted.

"Yes. I've always had security cameras. As it happens, I've just installed one of those doorbell cams at my son's request. He reckons they're brilliant. So, I thought I might as well buy one. You can't be too careful where security is concerned these days, can you?"

"Quite right. You mentioned that people have been coming and going at the property all day. Can you tell us more? Perhaps describe them?" Katy asked.

He cast his eye around the group, and then his gaze dropped on Katy again. "This young bloke in a suit has been coming here alone for a few days. I assumed he was interested and was probably measuring up for curtains or blinds, you know, doing the type of thing before you take over a place. Anyway, he showed up earlier with a much older man. I couldn't tell if he was tanned or if he was of ethnic origin. Anyway, they went in the house and stayed there for about ten minutes. They seemed pretty pleased with themselves when they came out of there, slapping each other on the back and sharing a few jokes as they made their way back to their cars."

"When was the last time anyone was here?"

"About thirty minutes ago, maybe an hour. I had just returned from my walk. There was a white van parked on the drive. I ran upstairs to have a nosey from the back bedroom. I thought someone was moving in, but I was wrong. Two blokes in overalls carried some rugs out of the house."

Lorne closed her eyes, but the image was running rampant through her mind. *What does that mean? That Charlie and the other girls are dead?*

Tony wrapped an arm around her shoulder. "I can tell what's going on in that head of yours. Stop overthinking things."

She opened her eyes and smiled at him. "I can't help it."

"Would you mind showing us the footage if you've caught these men on camera?" Katy asked. She peered over her shoulder and winked at Lorne.

"Yes, of course. If I can work out how to view the footage," the neighbour said.

"I can help with that," Stephen offered.

"What's your name, sir?" Katy asked.

"Geoff Styles. Come back to the house with me; we'll see what we can find. Don't mind Rex; he's a good boy. I made him bark at you—he's my protector. Some toerag robbed me in the street last year. He wouldn't have come near if I'd had Rex with me."

"Always good to have extra security on hand," Katy said.

He led the way back to his house. Katy, Lorne and Stephen joined him. He showed them through to a home office and pointed out the equipment he'd had installed.

"Wow, this is a neat setup," Stephen said.

"I'm glad you appreciate it, lad. Fill your boots; I haven't got a clue where to start with it. I'm going to feed Rex in the kitchen. Does anyone fancy a cuppa?"

Katy smiled but waved the suggestion away. "We're fine. We'll view the footage and get out of your hair soon."

"Take your time. All this is quite exciting for me. The days are long when you get to my age. I knew it was the wrong thing to do—retiring early. Everyone told me I was doing the right thing. I was an idiot to listen to them. Days are long and very mundane."

"Sorry to hear that," Katy replied. "Aren't you married?"

"No, the wife left me not long after I gave up work. She told me she couldn't put up with me hanging around the house all day, getting under her feet. Bloody cheek. That's when I started getting interested in this security lark. The problem was that once it was fitted, I found it all rather daunting. I'll leave you to it."

"Poor bloke," Lorne said. "Fancy living in a house this size and your wife buggers off."

"I'm surprised he hasn't been forced to sell up to give her half of it," Katy said. "Anyway, what can you do for us, Stephen?"

He took a seat and inspected the equipment thoroughly before jumping into action. "I think I've got it sussed. Give me five minutes and I should have a result for you. This is to the cameras surrounding the house."

He played the video, and the camera picked up the van, arriving at three-fifteen and leaving at three-forty. They watched in horror as the two burly men easily carried three rolled-up rugs into the house over their shoulders. However, it took both of them to carry each rug back out minutes later and load them into the rear of the van.

"I'd say there are definitely bodies in the rugs they brought out," Stephen said unnecessarily. "Sorry, I should have kept my mouth shut."

Lorne patted him on the shoulder. "No need to apologise. Can you get a close-up of either of the men and the registration number on the van? That'll be a start."

He zoomed in, and Katy jotted down the licence plate.

"I'll get Karen onto this right away." She withdrew her phone and gave Karen the information. "I'll stay on the line. It's a white Ford Transit."

"Nothing is coming up, boss. Must be a fake plate."

"Why am I not surprised to hear that? Okay, thanks, Karen. Can you try to locate it on the ANPRs and get back to me?"

"Leave it with me. I'll see what I can do."

Katy put her phone in her pocket. "Okay, we've seen enough of the goons. Geoff said that two men showed up earlier. Can you try to find them, Stephen?"

"On it now."

He rewound the disc until Nathan's car came on the screen.

Lorne felt physically sick when she saw it. "That's Nathan's. Looking at him makes my blood boil."

"I bet," Katy said. "Wait, who's this?"

They watched a rotund man in his fifties come out of the house. It was as Geoff said: the two men seemed pleased with themselves.

Katy peered over Stephen's shoulder. "To me, it seems like a deal has been done and they're congratulating each other."

"I think you're right," Lorne agreed. She spun around and struggled to fight back the tears. "I detest that man so much. You're going to have to restrain me when we catch up with the fucker. I'll gladly send him on his way to be reunited with his father."

Katy rubbed her arm. "You're going to have to stand in line for that one, love. Stephen, zoom in again and get both registration numbers, if you can."

Katy jotted down the numbers and immediately sent the information to Karen—this time via a text message. She instantly received a thumbs-up from the sergeant back at the station.

Geoff returned to the room just as they were about to leave. "I hope you've found what you're looking for."

"We have. You've been very helpful, Geoff. We can't thank you enough for allowing us into your home to view the footage."

His cheeks reddened. "Always a pleasure to assist the police. I don't think you're getting the credit you deserve at the moment as a Force."

"Thank you. That's kind of you to say so."

"Good luck with your operation. You never did tell me what's been going on in that house." He grinned. "Care to give me a hint?"

"We believe three women who were recently abducted have been held there."

"Oh, shit! Really? On my doorstep? That's unbelievable."

"I'm afraid so. Thanks again for your help. We'd better get off now."

"Well, I hope you find the bastards. We could do without their sort around here. This is a nice estate. We'd prefer to keep it that way."

"I'm sure. We'll do what we can to remedy this situation."

"Umm... just before we go, ma'am. You might want to take a look at this." Stephen highlighted the front of the van. "There's someone else inside."

"Can you get a closer look?"

He zoomed in, but the image was blurry. He pulled it back a little, and Lorne said, "It's him. Nathan was in the van with the goons."

"Okay. Let's go," Katy said.

They all flew past Geoff, who had pressed himself against the bookcase by the door.

"Thanks again, Geoff."

"You're welcome," he called after them. Rex started barking from the kitchen. "Shut up, boy. We're safe now."

"Let's hope he is," Lorne mumbled as they left the house.

"He'll be fine because by the end of the day, Nathan will be banged up in a cell," Katy assured her.

Katy let the rest of the team know what they had seen on the security cameras. "I've got Karen searching the ANPRs back at the station," she added.

"What's our next move?" Sean asked. "I've dismissed the Response Team. I didn't feel it was necessary for them to hang around. The commanding officer told me to call him if we need his assistance over the next day or two."

"Christ, I hope it doesn't take that long to find them," Lorne mumbled.

Katy gently punched her arm. "It won't. Look around you; we've got the A-Team on hand."

"I can't tell you how grateful I am to you all, especially you, Sally, for coming all the way down here to join us."

"Christ, I'd be gutted if I wasn't in on the action. Umm... that came out wrong, you know what I mean."

Lorne smiled. "It's great to have you by our side."

"Back to the station then, I presume," Sean said.

"Yes. There's nothing more we can do... except contact the estate agent who has this place up for sale," Katy said.

"Unless he's already bought it," Tony chipped in. "He told us the agent's name was Zach, if that helps."

Lorne nodded, confirming that Tony was right. "He shouldn't be hard to find. I'll search the internet on the way back and see what I can come up with."

The convoy set off towards the station. Lorne browsed through the list of agents in the immediate area and stumbled across one who might fit the bill. "I've got a Z Reynolds who owns Elite Properties. Hang on, his office is not far from here. It might be worth dropping in to ask him a few questions."

"I agree. Give me the address or tell me which roads to take. That'll be quicker. Lorne, can you call the others and let them know?" Katy passed her mobile through the seats.

Lorne handed Tony her phone so he could direct Katy to the location. Everything was running smoothly, like a well-oiled machine. When she rang the other members of the team, Sean and Graham, she suggested that they should go ahead and return to the station. But Sean was adamant they should stick together as one unit, just in case anything significant happened in the meantime.

Katy sighed once Lorne had filled her in. "I thought he'd question that order."

"C'est la vie," Lorne said.

"Take the next turning on the right," Tony ordered.

Katy indicated, and then followed the road to the end. The estate agent's office was on the corner.

"I think Lorne and I should take it from here," Katy said.

Tony and Carol agreed to remain in the car.

"Be careful. He's a sly bugger," Carol warned.

"Are you ready for this?" Katy asked as they climbed the steps to the office.

"Silly question. Bring it on."

When they entered the office, two of the agents were dealing with customers.

A young man at the back saw them enter and approached them with a broad smile. "Hello. What can I do for you, ladies?"

Katy's smile matched his. She presented her ID and said loudly, "We're here to see Zach Reynolds."

The two other agents and the customers they were dealing with all turned to face them.

"Is he expecting you?" the young agent asked.

"No, we've just called on the off-chance. We were in the area. Is he here?"

The agent peered over his shoulder at one of the other agents. The man excused himself from the customer and came towards them. "I'm Zach. What's this about?"

"Do you really want to have this conversation here?" Katy asked.

He frowned. "I'm not sure why you're here. I've got nothing to hide, but yes, I'd prefer to talk in my office." He faced the other agents. "Dan, can you deal with Mr and Mrs Carter for me?"

"We can come back," Mrs Carter said. She rose from her seat. "Come on, Harry. I think we should rethink our plans."

The couple left their seats, and the woman threw Zach a look of disgust as she passed them.

"Well, thanks for that. They were just about to make an offer on a five-million-pound house."

"And how is that our fault?" Katy challenged.

He walked away, mumbled something indecipherable, then shouted, "Are you coming? My time is valuable. Let's get this over with."

They followed him through to a plush office. He sat in his executive chair but didn't offer them a seat. "I'm waiting. Why have you come here today?"

"We believe you've recently been dealing with a Nathan Baldwin. Is that correct?"

"Dealing with? What are you insinuating?"

"It was a simple question."

"I know Nathan. What about him?"

"Has he bought the property he was interested in? The one in Cromer Crescent?"

"No, he's noted an interest in the property and has held on to the keys while he obtains several quotes from builders."

"I see," Katy replied. "Are you in the habit of allowing customers to keep hold of the keys to a property of that value?"

"No. But Nathan is a friend of mine."

"Ah, okay. And do you trust him?"

"What a ridiculous question. Why wouldn't I? We've been friends for years."

"Ah, but how well do you really know him?"

"Well enough. What the hell is going on here? Why are you questioning me about Nathan? What's he been up to?"

"Quite a lot. Mostly, this past week he's abducted three women, and one of them happens to be my partner. That's right—a serving police officer. You look shocked to hear that."

His eyes darted to the right. Lorne prepared herself, sensing he was about to jump out of his seat and attempt to escape out of the door that led to a courtyard.

"Don't even think about it. We have the property surrounded," Katy warned. "If you try to run, all you'll be doing is proving you're involved in the abductions."

"I'm not. This is the first I've heard about it. You have to believe me. What does this have to do with me?"

"Hmm... let me think? Ah, yes, we could be here because Nathan has been holding the women in the cellar at the manor house in Cromer Crescent. You know the one, the house you gave him the keys to. You see, some officers might arrest you for aiding and abetting criminal activity, but not me. No, I can tell you're keen to help us, rather than spend the rest of the day in a police cell. Would I be right in thinking that, Zach?"

"Yes. I promise, I didn't have a clue what he was doing at the house. He's lied to me. If he'd told me what his intentions were, I would never have given him the key. He's duped me into believing that he was going to buy that property. As a friend, I gave him the first option of buying it. I have other customers begging to see that house. I'm horrified that he's used me in this way."

Katy glanced sideways at Lorne, who shrugged.

"Are you willing to make up for your mistake?" Lorne asked.

"Yes, yes, please give me the opportunity to do that. What can I do to help?"

"Give us Nathan's contact details: his address and phone number."

"What? Of course." He grabbed his phone off the desk and scrolled through his contacts. Then he passed the phone to Katy, who noted the information down.

"Can we trust you not to tip him off?" Katy looked up from her notebook to ask.

"What? Yes, absolutely. I'm a successful businessman with an impeccable reputation to uphold in this part of the city. I want nothing more to do with Nathan."

"If he rings you, will you call me right away? Here's my card."

"Absolutely. You have my word. I feel like shit right now, knowing that he's deceived me." He shook his head. "Those poor women. Have you been to the house?"

Katy nodded. "Yes. We've just come from there. It was empty when we broke in. Ah, yes, you're going to need to repair the door. That's another reason why we dropped by to have a word with you." Her mobile rang. She apologised and turned her back on Lorne and Zach. "Shit! Okay, we're on our way. Thanks, Karen. Could you arrange for a patrol car to go to Cromer Crescent to ensure that no one enters the manor house? We're with the agent now. He's aware of the damage caused by the Armed Response Team. I'll be in touch soon."

"We need to go." Katy pointed at Zach. "If we find out that you've tipped Nathan off, we'll have no other option but to arrest you for being his accomplice in the abductions. For your information, the crime carries a five- to ten-year stretch in prison."

"Are you kidding me? I'm innocent, I swear I am. Why the fu… the hell, would I jeopardise all of this? I've built this business from scratch. I wouldn't, I promise."

"We'll leave you to it. If he contacts you, ring me ASAP. Don't let on that you've spoken to us. You'll only be putting yourself in danger. He's the type who prefers to tidy up loose ends."

"What's that supposed to mean? Fuck, I was doing a friend a favour, end of. I would never have chosen to get involved in something as obscene as this. You have to believe me."

"I'm still on the fence about your involvement. What you do from now on will tell us all we need to know about your relationship with Nathan. I'm going to put a plainclothes officer on duty outside. If you try to leave to warn Nathan, I'll give the officer instructions to arrest you right away. Am I making myself clear?"

His hands trembled, and he clasped them together in front of him. "Perfectly clear. I have no intention of contacting Nathan again. I can do without shit like this landing on my doorstep."

"Good. Thanks for the information." Katy waved her notebook.

He left his seat, and they followed him back to the entrance.

Katy shook his hand and whispered. "Don't forget, we're watching you. Oh, and I forgot to mention that we'll be alerted if you try to call him, so I'd think twice about doing that the second we leave."

"I don't know how many more times I have to tell you. I want nothing more to do with him. In fact, I hope you find the bastard and bang him up for life."

Katy smiled, then she and Lorne left the building.

"Don't laugh. Hold it together until we get in the car. He'll be watching us."

"You're an evil woman when you want to be, Katy Foster."

"I had the best teacher."

Before they got in the car, they both peered over their shoulders and saw Zach standing at the front door of the office, looking at them.

They entered the car and burst into laughter. Once they'd calmed down, Katy made her way back to the station while Lorne filled Carol and Tony in on what had just happened.

Carol chuckled. "I bet he was crapping himself. I can't see him contacting Nathan now."

"Me neither. What about the information he's given you? Isn't that worth chasing up? Is it different to what we have on him already?"

"I'll check when we get back to the station. We can get a trace put on his phone and request the call information from the provider," Katy replied.

Lorne glanced over her shoulder at Sean and Graham, still following them. "Maybe it would be better to stay out in the field. There's a lay-by up ahead. Why don't we see what Sean thinks?"

"I don't mind. I'll pull in."

Katy and Lorne got out of the vehicle, and the rest of the team, including Sally, joined them. Carol and Tony wound their windows down so they could also join in.

"How did it go back there?" Sean was the first to ask.

Katy revealed what had happened with Zach.

Sean blew out a breath. "And you trust him? Maybe you should have brought him in and kept him in a cell until Nathan has been caught."

"Don't worry, I think I put the fear of God in him. The last thing he's going to do is jeopardise his business. I told him we had an officer watching the agency and monitoring any calls that might be made from the premises."

Sean winked and wagged a finger. "Smart move."

"I also received a call from Karen to say that uniform have found Nathan's vehicle."

"Where?" Sean asked.

"In a car park close to the manor house."

"We saw him in the van with the two thugs," Lorne said. "So that makes sense."

"What we need is a sighting of the van on the ANPRs," Katy said. "Until we've got that, there's nothing we can do for now. Not unless Carol can come to our rescue."

Carol's mouth turned down. "There's something forming, but I wouldn't know where to begin. All I'm seeing is the girls in darkness."

"I agree. That's not going to help us find them. Could they still be wrapped up in the rugs which left the house?" Lorne asked. "Dare I ask... if they're still alive?"

"They're all alive," Carol confirmed. "Pete's with them. At the moment, he's being as much use as a fart in a colander, but I wouldn't dare tell him that."

They all laughed and returned to their respective vehicles, then drove back to the station. When they arrived, they got to work. Tony and Carol made themselves useful by making everyone a drink and handing them around.

It didn't take Carol long to draw Lorne's attention.

"What's wrong, Carol?" Lorne jabbed Katy in the arm, and they both crossed the room to speak to her.

"Something is coming. Yes, there is a lot of light around the women now. They're all okay, badly bruised, but Charlie is doing her best to raise their spirits. Where are they, Pete? Describe their surroundings to us, please."

The room fell silent, and the team gathered around.

Sally clutched Lorne's arm. "She's got this, Lorne. Have faith in her abilities."

Lorne nodded and rested her forehead against Sally's until Carol sat upright in her chair and began rocking back and forth.

"I see large containers," Carol said. She squeezed her eyes shut.

"Can you describe them, Carol?" Lorne asked after a few moments of silence.

"Large metal containers. There's water lapping at walls. Wait, I hear heavy machinery moving, with beepers sounding as they reverse."

Graham wrote something down in his notebook and showed it to Lorne.

"Yes," she mouthed to him and handed the notebook around to the others. "Could it be a dock, Carol? Are there boats being loaded?"

"Yes, I think so. The image isn't clear enough. Wait, the girls have been plunged into darkness again. They're clinging together. Men standing around, patting each other on the back."

Lorne's heart rate increased. "Carol, can you give us anything else about the dock? There are several close by. If we turn up at the wrong one, we could lose them forever."

"I'm trying. So is Pete. Come on, man, look around you. Tell me what you see. Or can you hear the men talking? Give us a hint as to what they're saying." Carol nodded and opened her eyes. "Get me a map."

Stephen crossed the room and unpinned the large map from the noticeboard. He spread it out on the desk next to Carol and pointed out where the station was. "We're here. We've got docks on either side of the Thames all along the river."

"Do you know which ones are the most popular for exporting, Graham?"

"What about the West India Docks here? It's not too far from us."

Carol stared at the map for what seemed like an eternity. "Pete, come back. Where are you?" She sighed and placed her head in her hands. "His strength is waning. I think the last investigation took a lot out of both of us. No, wait, he's back again. What's that? Can you repeat it? The container has a number on it. He's trying to find it."

"Come on, Pete, we're relying on you. Charlie needs you to assist her," Lorne whispered.

"Okay, I'll let them know. He's telling me that there's an 836SA, plus other numbers and letters thrown into the mix. He thinks it should help you locate the container. We have to be quick. Time is running out for the girls."

THE CONVOY GOT on the road again. This time they headed across London towards the dock. Sean asked Sally to drive his car while he made the necessary calls to flood the area with police.

Lorne was relieved that Sean was taking her daughter's plight seriously. It hadn't always been the case when they were chasing Nathan's father, when he'd kidnapped Charlie. She couldn't help wondering how Charlie was holding up under the pressure.

"What are you thinking?" Katy asked.

"How Charlie is coping. They must have drugged the girls before rolling them in the rugs. I'm hoping it will wear off so Charlie can defend herself, if she's able."

"We're better off not dealing with ifs and maybes, darling," Tony said. "Let's hope we can get to the docks before…"

Lorne raised her hand. "Don't say it."

"She's going to be fine, Lorne," Carol assured her. "None of us will allow the men to hurt her."

Lorne wasn't so sure. There were dozens of questions bombarding her mind. *What if we arrive too late? SA—could that be South Africa? How long will they be stuck in the container if we don't rescue them? How much air do they have in the container? There have been numerous reports lately of immigrants dying in the backs of lorries coming from France, a relatively short trip in comparison.*

Tony nudged her. "Give your mind a rest. It's only going to make things ten times worse."

She smiled and blew out a breath. "I can't help it. SA... that could be South Africa; if it's not their destination, where else could it be?"

"Stop torturing yourself. We're almost there. Hopefully, the container will still be on the dock."

"And if it's not? What happens once it gets loaded onto a ship? Do we still have the authority to search the vessel?"

"Of course we do. It's still within our boundaries. Now, stop worrying."

"Easier said than done."

He held her hand tightly and then kissed the back of it. "No one is going to let Charlie down, not this time."

"He's right, Lorne," Katy agreed. She turned left at the lights.

Ahead of them, the docks came into view. As they got closer, Lorne heaved out another sigh.

"Shit, it's going to be like searching for the proverbial needle amongst this lot."

Ahead of them were row upon row of containers. Several mobile cranes were on hand, loading the containers onto the waiting ships. Lorne's head swivelled in all directions, and her heart sank at the mammoth task that she suspected lay ahead of them.

"I'm going to park up here. I think that's the office over to the right. Tony, why don't you come with me? I've got a feeling we'll get more information out of the workers if a man is present."

"I hate to say this, Katy, but I believe you might be right." He pecked Lorne on the lips. "We'll be right back."

They left the car.

Carol turned in her seat and reached for Lorne's hand. "Stay strong. If she's still here, we'll find her, Lorne."

"Is Pete still around?"

Carol shook her head. "No. His spirit was too weak; he needs to re-energise his power. He should be back with us soon."

"I hope so. We need him. Are you picking up on anything, Carol? Any of the containers drawing you to them?"

"Disappointingly, I have to admit it's not happening, not yet."

Sean opened the back door of the car, startling Lorne.

She placed a hand over her chest. "Jesus, don't sneak up on me like that."

He laughed. "I wasn't aware that I had. I just dropped by to tell you that Graham, Stephen and I are going to scour the area."

"Is that wise? Shouldn't we all stick together? That was your suggestion earlier," Lorne reminded him.

He tutted. "Wise-arse. Sally, why don't you jump in the back with Lorne? We won't be long."

Sally opened the other back door and jumped in beside Lorne. Sean joined up with Graham and Stephen and walked towards the ships being loaded.

"I volunteered to go with them, but Sean wouldn't hear of it."

"Don't take it personally; he's always been a misogynistic prick. Oops, excuse my language, Carol."

Carol sniggered. "You're excused and you're also right. His attitude to you over the years has been appalling."

"Don't worry; I can handle him. I've dealt with his sort before—many times over the years."

Tony and Katy returned to the car, both looking perplexed.

"The guy showed us the manifest. We went through it a dozen times, but we couldn't find a container with those numbers or letters on it, and there was nothing booked to travel to South Africa today."

"Shit! What does that mean?" Lorne asked. She answered her own question before anyone else had the chance to do so. "That we're at the wrong docks?"

Suddenly, what sounded like gunfire broke out ahead of them.

"What the fuck is going on?" Katy said. She withdrew her Taser. "Stay here, take cover behind the manager's office if things get bad."

"I'm coming with you." Lorne tore out of the car before anyone could stop her.

"If Lorne is going, then so am I," Sally announced.

"Shit, ladies," Katy said. "You've got me by the short and curlies. We don't have time to debate the issue. Get your weapons ready. Tony, why don't you take Carol to the manager's office and lock yourselves in?"

Tony pulled a face. It was obvious he was eager to take part in the action that was about to kick off, but he also knew his limitations, given that he had a prosthetic limb to contend with.

Several cars screeched to a halt behind them. Reinforcements had arrived in the form of uniformed officers. Katy approached the men to make them aware of the situation. Then she made a call on her mobile. When she joined Sally and Lorne back at the car, Lorne asked, "Who did you call?"

"The commanding officer of the Armed Response Team. They're on their way."

"Glad to hear it. The Tasers are going to be useless against their weapons," Lorne agreed.

More shots rang out.

"This way." Katy took the lead and, with their Tasers at the ready, the three of them ran for cover behind the containers in front of them.

In the distance, they could hear Sean Roberts shouting for the criminals to put their weapons down. More shots sounded to their right. From their position, they saw two men with guns appear fifty feet ahead of them. Their attention was not drawn by Lorne, Katy and Sally, but by something else in the other direction.

"We could sneak up on them," Sally whispered.

"That's what I was thinking," Lorne replied. "What do you think, Katy?"

"I'm not so sure. They've got guns."

"And we've got Tasers, with the added upper hand because they haven't seen us."

Charlie strained an ear. There was no doubt in her mind that they had just heard gunfire. "We need to keep calm. I don't think it will be long now."

"What do you mean?" Isla asked, her eyes widening with fear.

"I think the police are here. They have to be."

"What if the criminals are having a shoot-out among themselves?" Davina added. "What if one lot has double-crossed the others and… oh, I don't know, I could be talking a lot of shit. You're the detective, after all."

Suddenly, they were thrown from one side of the container to the other. Charlie had the foresight to raise her hands to prevent herself from hitting the wall. She watched the other two girls whack their heads against the wall and knock themselves out. The movement continued. Charlie ran the length of the container, searching for a spyhole. She found a small one at the rear. She gasped when she saw that they were around a hundred feet off the ground. Then her stomach dipped, telling her that the container was being lowered. She didn't have to be a genius to know that they were being loaded onto a ship.

She banged on the container, hoping to attract someone's attention below them. Charlie continued to bang until her hands and fists started to bleed. Tears slipped from her eyes, her fate out of her hands. It was a horrible feeling to deal with, especially as the vile memories she had managed to suppress over the years were now sitting prominently at the front of her mind. She put her hands together and winced, then she said a little prayer, hoping they would be saved before they set sail to God knows where.

The three women were halfway towards their targets, their Tasers raised, ready to fire at a moment's notice.

The men were unaware of their presence, their weapons also ready for action. They were concentrating on what lay ahead of them.

"Drop your weapons," Katy shouted, "or we'll fire."

The men dropped their guns. Both shouted an expletive and slowly faced them.

"They're the two goons who removed the rugs from the house," Lorne whispered in Katy's ear.

"Yep. Turn around," she ordered. "Put your hands behind your back. Do it. Now."

The men carried out her instructions to perfection until the man closest to the opening made a run for it.

"I've got him," Lorne said and took off after him, leaving Sally and Katy to cuff the other goon.

Lorne shouted for the man to stop. When he refused, Lorne aimed her Taser. It crossed her mind that he might be out of range. As it turned out, he wasn't, and he dropped to the ground as fifty thousand volts surged through him. Two uniformed officers appeared at her side. She left them to deal with the suspect and returned to Katy and Sally, who had cuffed his associate and were in the process of handing him over to another couple of uniformed officers.

"We're one weapon short now," Katy said.

Lorne thought quickly on her feet and asked one of the officers for his Taser. He hesitated, knowing that he could get in trouble.

"I'll take the blame, I promise. This is urgent."

The male officer nodded and unclipped his Taser. "Let's hope you don't have to use it."

"Don't worry, it'll be used as a last resort," Katy assured him. She led the way.

They crept to the end of the row of containers for a better look at what was going on ahead of them. More gunfire drew their attention as they repositioned.

"Can you tell where it's coming from?" Sally asked.

"I think that way," Katy said. She pointed ahead of them. As the coast was clear, Katy crossed the divide between the two rows for a better view. She peered around the container and quickly pulled her head back. She held up two fingers and mouthed, "Two more goons ahead of us."

"Can we sneak up on them?" Lorne mouthed back, in return.

Katy tutted. "I think it would be too dangerous." She glanced down at her feet and saw a collection of stones. "I could use these to distract one of them, draw him away from the other one."

Lorne and Sally both nodded and raised their Tasers, prepared for every eventuality as Katy lobbed the stones. They clattered against the container opposite.

"What the fuck was that?" one of the goons said.

"I'll check it out," the other one shouted.

Katy, Lorne and Sally pressed themselves against the container until they heard footsteps coming closer. Katy was the first to break cover, with Lorne and Sally close behind her. Katy fired her Taser. The man cried out and instantly dropped to the ground.

The other man saw them and turned to run.

"He's mine," Sally shouted and fired the Taser.

The man writhed around on the ground for a few minutes before Sally let go of the trigger. She stood over him and slapped on the cuffs. Two more uniformed officers arrived and dealt with the wires.

"Another successful operation," Katy said.

Lorne shook her head. "I wouldn't get too cocky if I were you."

Another shot sounded just ahead of them. They followed the noise, keeping close to the containers.

"We've got you surrounded now," Sean said. "Your men have all deserted you, Nathan. It's time for you to call it a day."

"Never. I'll go down fighting if I have to, just like my father."

Out of view, Lorne muttered, "Bloody idiot. If only he knew what a coward his father had been at the end of his life, without his men there to protect him."

"We need to be cautious. We need to get the information out about him of where he's holding Charlie and the other two women."

"I've got a sense that it's too late. Look at this place; it was a hive of activity when we arrived. How do we know they haven't been loaded onto a vessel by now and set sail?" Lorne replied.

"Stop thinking negatively. We've got this, Lorne. We'll put a halt to the operations around here if it's called for. First, we have to capture Nathan without injuring him."

"That won't be easy," Sally chipped in.

"Easier than you think. He seems panicked to me, as though he senses we're closing in on him and that his men are dropping like flies around him," Katy said. "Are you ready, ladies? I think we should grab this bastard by the... I'll leave the rest of that sentence to your imagination. I'm going to need a weapon."

Sally handed hers over.

Katy inched closer to the voices with Lorne and Sally behind her.

At the end of the row, she peered around the container and quickly dipped back again. "He's there, standing out in the open as if challenging those around him."

"We can take him down with the element of surprise. We needn't show ourselves. Just fire the Taser at him. Even if it hits his leg, it'll be enough to put him off his stride, allowing the others to take advantage of him," Lorne said. "I'm up for taking the shot. In fact, nothing would give me greater satisfaction."

Katy nodded, and they switched places. Quietly, Lorne shuffled closer to the end of the container and peered around it. Nathan was standing twenty feet away from her, holding a gun by his side.

"The arrogant shit. I'll show him." She fired the Taser.

It found its target, and he sank to the ground, dropping his weapon.

Everyone broke cover and raced towards him. Lorne refused to stop the charge until his weapon had been collected.

Sean had to nudge her to remind her, "It's over, Lorne. Release your finger."

Lorne was in a daze. All she could think about was the danger Charlie was in. She kicked Nathan in the side and shouted, "Where's Charlie? What have you done to her?"

Nathan was hoisted to his feet by Stephen and Graham.

He looked Lorne up and down and spat at her feet. "You'll never find her. That was the whole purpose of this exercise: to kidnap her and take her away from you. You'll spend the rest of your life wondering where she is." He let out a sinister laugh.

Lorne flew at him, her fists clenched. She punched him several times before Sean could pull her away.

"Stop it. We'll find her."

"In your dreams," Nathan shouted over his shoulder as Graham and Stephen led him away.

Lorne sobbed as the fear descended, and Sean gathered her in his arms. She cried against his chest.

Katy and Sally rubbed her back.

"Don't give up on her, Lorne," Sally pleaded. "She's resilient, just like her mother."

Lorne pushed away from Sean when she spotted Tony and Carol coming around the corner. "Any news, Carol?"

"I might have something. I'm sensing the container has just been loaded onto a ship."

Lorne took off towards the dock, the rest of them close on her tail. At the edge of the dock, she cast her eyes around the ships being loaded. At a glance, she spotted four of them. She searched for the names, and then it dawned on her. "That one over there. It's registered in Saudi Arabia."

"Shit!" Sean said. "We were looking for the wrong ship. Let me see what I can do to prevent it from leaving." He set off like a greyhound out of the traps.

Carol hooked her arm through Lorne's and whispered, "She's going to be okay."

Lorne smiled and patted her good friend's hand. "I hope so. I couldn't bear to lose her, not under these circumstances. Who knows what that bastard has lined up for her? Saudi Arabia... we have to intervene. Her life wouldn't be worth living if she ended up there."

"She won't," Tony said adamantly. "We've got this. She's around here somewhere. We just have to find her."

Stephen and Graham rejoined the group.

"Where is he?" Lorne demanded to know.

"In the back of a police van, on his way to the station," Graham replied. "Boss," he turned to Katy and said, "The ART has arrived."

Katy sighed. "I'm not sure if we need them."

"I think it would be wise to have them around until we find Charlie and the others," Tony advised her.

"Tony's right. What harm can it do?" Sally asked.

"I'd better go back and see them to make them aware of what we're up against. I'll leave it up to the commanding officer to make the decision," Katy said and headed back to where they had parked the cars.

Carol remained quiet. Lorne took a step towards her.

"They're all okay. Two of them were knocked out when the container was lifted, but Charlie wasn't. Her determination will see her through, Lorne."

10

The door of the container eased back, and three foreign men stood at the opening, staring at them. When one of them spoke, it wasn't in English. He grew frustrated when Charlie and the other two women remained where they were, staring at him.

His two associates entered the container and dragged Isla and Davina onto the deck of the ship by their hair.

Charlie held her hands up. "I'll come peacefully. You don't have to hurt any of us."

The main man got behind her and pushed her, sending her off-balance. She barged into the other girls.

"Stay calm, just do as they say for now," Charlie whispered.

One man stayed ahead of them. They were ordered to follow him down some steps below decks. Charlie was tempted to shout out for help, but what would be the use? The machinery working around the dock would drown out any cries for help.

What are they going to do with us belowdecks?

They were taken to a cabin with three beds, and the door was locked behind them. Charlie tore over to the small window and tried to open it. It was locked, and there was no sign of it budging, no matter how much Charlie tugged at it.

"Where do you think they're taking us?" Isla asked. She sat on the bed and clutched her arms around her legs.

"I have no idea. All we can do is keep alert. Hopefully, we'll be rescued before we set sail."

"And if we aren't?" Davina snapped back.

Charlie shrugged. "I don't want to think that far ahead. I've always dealt with issues as they come up. It's how I work."

"What if we set sail? Where do you think we'll end up?" Isla asked.

"I don't know. I struggled to make out what language they were speaking."

"They look like they're Arabs to me," Davina said. "We had a few Arabs in our class at university."

"Yes, you're right," Isla agreed. "Oh no, God help us. I don't want to end up there. Charlie, please, you have to do something to save us."

"I'm trying. Believe me, the last thing we need is for this ship to set sail." She peered out of the window. All she could see was the end of the dock and the vast expanse of sea ahead of them. Charlie resisted the temptation to shudder and began pacing the floor as she thought of a way out. If it came to the crunch, she was a black belt in karate. If she felt their lives were in danger, she'd have no hesitation using her combat skills to save them. Until now, she'd thought it would be wiser to keep her capabilities to herself. However, now she was wondering if she had done the right thing.

"What are you thinking?" Isla asked.

"I'm trying to work out how we can get ourselves out of this mess without drawing attention to ourselves. There are bound to be dozens of crew members on board a vessel of this size."

Davina gasped. "You think we should risk it? Try to overpower whoever comes to see us?"

Charlie nodded. "It depends on the numbers. If one man shows up, then it'll be three against one in our favour."

Isla shrugged. "I'm up for it. I'm pretty fit. I go to the gym quite a lot."

Davina smiled and held her clenched fist in the air. "Girl power! I like the idea of that. I go to the gym, too. Granted, not as often as I should, but I'm stronger than they're likely to think I am."

"Okay, as long as they don't drug us, we should remain alert at all times."

﹏

Sean returned with the ART. "We're good to go. Jack and his team are going to board the vessel. The manager finally admitted that the ship is due to set sail in twenty minutes."

"Don't worry. Leave it to us," Jack said.

The group moved to a clearing close to the dock, and they clung to each other while the ART stormed the ship. Gunshots rang out again; it was obvious that the crew were prepared to go down fighting.

Lorne's hand covered her mouth, and her body trembled during the raid. Tony held her close and whispered reassuring words in her ear throughout.

"I can't stand this. What if they've dumped their bodies overboard?" she sobbed.

"Lorne, stop it. I'm not sensing anything has gone wrong... yet," Carol said. She slipped an arm around Lorne's waist and rested her head on her shoulder.

"What can you see, Carol, if anything?"

"I'm not. Pete is with her. Take heart from that, love. He won't let her come to any harm."

"I hope you're right."

The team had cleared the threat on the deck, and the commanding officer gave a thumbs-up before he and his men entered the bowels of the ship.

"Oh God, I hope they find them soon. I don't think I can take much more of this," Lorne mumbled.

Gunshots sounded, and everyone sucked in a breath.

The next ten minutes seemed to stretch into hours. Lorne stood away from Tony and Carol, needing the space to pace the area. Drops of rain splattered on her face. "That's all we need."

"We should take cover," Katy suggested.

"You go. I'm staying right here."

The heavens opened, and the others dived for cover, but Lorne insisted she needed to stay put despite Tony trying to tug on her arm.

If anything, she inched closer to the ship. A shot rang out and hit the ground inches from her feet that sent her diving for cover behind a nearby van. She peered over her shoulder to see Tony shaking his head and fist at her.

Moments later, the only noise she could hear was the sound of the cranes and the forklift trucks in the distance. Lorne poked her head around the front of the van to see two members of the team bringing a couple of prisoners ashore. They passed them over to the awaiting uniformed officers and returned to the ship before Lorne had the chance to ask them what was going on and if the hostages were safe.

Another two prisoners were escorted off the ship and again handed over. Lorne's nerves tightened. She was aware that she needed to remain where she was, allowing the operation to play out before her.

TEN MINUTES LATER, she broke cover and ran towards the ship. Charlie and the two women walked down the gangplank, dressed in hessian sacks, while two armed officers—one at the front and the other at the rear—ensured they reached the shore safely.

"Charlie, are you all right?" Lorne asked, tears streaming down her cheeks. She smothered her daughter's face with kisses.

"Mum, I'm fine. We all are. Where's Nathan? Don't tell me he got away!"

"No. He'll be back at the station by now. Don't worry, he'll get what's coming to him. How are you all? Do any of you need medical care?"

"No. We're okay. We'd love to get out of this rain, though."

"Of course. I'm sorry. The cars are by the entrance. I'll see if Tony and Sean can bring them round."

It was Graham and Stephen who ran back to fetch the cars.

"How are you, Sergeant?" Sean asked.

"We survived. I don't mind admitting that we had our doubts now and again. He's drugged us several times over the past few days. He changed. I didn't know him at all. This was all about him seeking revenge for what had happened to his father in the past."

"It's over with now. Don't worry, we'll make him pay for his crimes. And how are you, ladies? No doubt you're eager to get home to your families. Are you sure you don't want to go to hospital to get checked over?"

Isla and Davina looked drained after their experience.

"I don't think we need to go to the hospital," Davina said. "All we need now is for you to tell us that Nathan isn't going to get off on a technicality. Money talks—we're aware of that."

"He won't. We'll ensure that doesn't happen, you have my assurance," Sean replied.

EPILOGUE

Katy had arranged for the duty doctor to call at the station to give the women a quick check before sending them home. She ensured Nathan had been processed and found the doctor already waiting for them in the reception area.

She returned to the cars to tell the team. The men went ahead of them, and the female officers, along with Carol, led Isla and Davina into the station. They were given some clothes, and then cleared to leave. Katy asked the desk sergeant to sort out a lift for the women.

"We can't thank you enough for all you've done for us," Isla said, speaking on behalf of Davina.

"We're going to need a statement from each of you," Katy said. "There's no rush, over the next few days will do."

"Of course. We want to see that man get the punishment he deserves," Davina said.

"So do we."

"I hope Charlie is going to be okay. She was amazing. She kept us calm throughout. Without her by our sides, I dread to think how this would have turned out," Isla said, her eyes filling up with fresh tears.

Davina wrapped an arm around her shoulder. "I agree. She's a very brave young woman, considering how that bastard treated her. Most women would have crumbled in that situation."

"She's one of the best," Katy said. "We'll be in touch soon, ladies. Take care of yourselves. Try not to let this encounter blight your lives."

"Hard not to, Katy, but we're going to do our best, aren't we, Davina?"

"Yes. Otherwise, the bastard will still be winning, won't he?" Davina replied.

"That's the spirit. I can tell you both have strong resolves." Katy showed them back out to the reception area and left them with the desk sergeant.

"Leave them with me, ma'am."

She punched in her passcode and walked up the stairs, her legs complaining with every step she took.

When she entered the main office, she sensed the atmosphere was a bit subdued. "Hey, what's all this? We should be celebrating a job well done, folks."

Lorne fixed Katy a mug of coffee. "Here you go. I think we're all feeling a little reflective. You know, considering what might have happened to Charlie and the other women if we hadn't found them."

"And that's my point. This is cause for a celebration. Charlie, Isla and Davina have been downstairs singing your praises. You're an amazing officer and young woman; you kept your cool when the odds were against you. I'm going to make sure DCI Roberts puts you forward for a commendation."

Charlie shook her head. "I don't need it. We're all free, that's all the gratitude I need. Anyway, if you lovely people hadn't shown up when you did... well, there's no need to finish that sentence, is there? So, what happens next?"

"I think you should go home and get some rest. Leave Nathan to us to interview; you shouldn't be part of that process anyway. Don't worry, he won't worm his way out of this, I assure you."

"I hope not, but then we all know that money talks. Let's be honest: if he's got his father's genes and, more importantly, his contacts, who knows who will be on his side once the case is heard in court?"

"No way. We won't allow that to happen, Charlie, so get any thoughts like that out of your head," Lorne chipped in.

"Your mum is right. There's no point thinking that way. We'll make sure everything goes smoothly; we'll dot every I and cross every T, double-checking and triple-checking every piece of evidence to ensure the case is watertight against him."

The phone rang in Katy's office. She patted Charlie's hand. "Have faith in us and the system, I know it's not easy at times." She ran to answer it and let out a scream.

Lorne and Sally appeared in the doorway.

"What's wrong?" Lorne demanded to know.

"It's Nathan; he's killed himself."

The team raced back downstairs. Charlie was a few feet ahead of them. She arrived in the cell first. The desk sergeant blocked her path.

"He's gone, Charlie."

"How?"

"He must have had a cyanide pill on him."

"Fucking bastard, fucking coward..." Charlie crumbled to her knees.

Lorne crouched beside her and rocked her like a baby. "Oh, love, I'm so sorry."

Katy offered them both a tissue. "May he rot in Hell alongside that vile father of his."

"Even Hell is too good for him," Sally said. "I'm so sorry he won't see the punishment he deserves, Charlie."

Carol stood at the back in silence.

LORNE SPOTTED her good friend and stood to speak with her. "Carol, are you okay?"

She shook her head. "No. I've let you all down. I should have seen this coming and warned you."

"Don't be silly. You're exhausted. You could never let us down. The danger was over. You led us to where Charlie was being kept. If you hadn't done that for us... we might never have seen Charlie and the other two women again."

Tears splattered on Carol's cheeks. "No matter what you say, I will always feel a failure. He deserved to be put in prison. I should have known he would try something like this."

"If you're apportioning blame, then it's our fault. He should have been searched thoroughly before he was put in the cell. But we won't go down that route. What's done is done. It's time for us to move on. Charlie and the other two women are safe, and now the world is free from yet another sick, twisted criminal."

Carol nodded. "You always were good at turning a negative into a positive, weren't you, Lorne?"

"I learnt many years ago to always accept what life has mapped out for us and to always look on the bright side."

"What's this?" Katy joined the conversation.

"Carol is blaming herself for what Nathan has done."

Katy gripped Carol's hand. "What nonsense that is. Criminals like him will always find a way to avoid going to jail. He would have been checked rigorously before being locked up. He must have hidden the pill in some orifice or other. Personally, I'd rather not delve too much into my imagination to come up with an answer for that one. This is no one's fault. He was determined to end his life. If it hadn't been here, he wouldn't have lasted long in prison and would have done the deed within a few days there instead. His type is used to the finer things in life. When that's stripped away from them, then it's simple, there's only one way out for them."

Carol nodded. "Okay, thank you for that."

Lorne pulled Katy away from the crowd and said, "We should visit his mother and tell her the news before it appears in the media."

"Christ, yes, I never thought about that. Let's get everyone organised and then shoot over there. You will come with me, won't you?"

"I think it should be down to you, Sally and I to tackle the task."

"What? No men as backup?"

"I don't think it'll be needed. That's my opinion, but it's your decision, Katy."

"Okay. I'm willing to go along with you. Perhaps we should have a patrol car on standby in case they're needed."

"I agree," Sally said.

Katy helped Lorne to get Charlie on her feet again. "Charlie, I think you should go back home with Carol and Tony," she suggested.

"No. I have work to do here."

"No. You need to go home and get some rest, but you shouldn't be alone," Katy insisted.

"Aren't you coming, Mum?"

"No. Katy has asked me and Sally to stick around and help with the paperwork on this investigation, darling."

Charlie's eyes narrowed. "I don't believe you but I'm too tired to argue. Stay safe, whatever you're up to."

Lorne smiled and kissed her daughter on the cheek. "You're too smart for your own good sometimes. Don't worry about us; we'll be fine. Sally and I won't be long, I promise."

OLIVIA BALDWIN LIVED in the country out in Surrey. Her mansion stood in its own grounds and was secured by a gated entrance.

"Here goes," Katy said. She left the car and pressed the buzzer.

As soon as she announced her identity, the gates slowly opened.

Katy jumped back into the car. "Well, that was easier than I anticipated."

"Let's hope the rest of the visit goes as smoothly as the gates opening," Lorne said.

Sally reached through the seats and gripped her arm. "We've got this."

Lorne patted her hand. "I know. I'm so glad to be going on this mission with my two favourite partners."

They all laughed.

Then Sally said, "Let's hope your other partner in spirit is with us, too."

With that, a rabbit ran out in front of them, causing Katy to slam on the brakes.

"He's here," Lorne whispered.

The drive was at least three hundred feet long. The lawn on either side of them was immaculately kept. Every now and then, they passed a tree dotting the lawn. Behind the Georgian mansion was a wooded area. All in all, the setting was impressive.

"Why wasn't this place seized when they collected The Unicorn's assets?" Sally asked.

"I bet she bought this with the money he had secretly stashed away. My guess is that she left it five or ten years before she splashed out on this place, just to avoid answering any awkward questions," Lorne suggested.

"So not right," Katy replied. She drew up outside the steps to the mansion. "Christ, I've seen it all now," she muttered as a well-suited butler opened the door to greet them.

"Are you ready for this?" Lorne asked.

"Bring it on," Katy and Sally said in unison.

They exited the car and ascended the steps.

"The lady of the house awaits you, ladies. She's in the drawing room. I've been instructed to ask you if you would care to take tea with the mistress."

"No, we're fine, thanks," Katy spoke for all of them. "We're here on official business."

"I see. In that case, I'll take you to the mistress."

He walked into the house, and Lorne pulled a face behind his back.

The interior was as grand as the exterior, with marble floors and stunning original artwork displayed throughout the ground floor.

Olivia Baldwin was elegantly seated on the sofa next to a roaring fire in the grate below the ornate mantelpiece. "Come in, ladies. I was surprised to learn you were here. How can I help?"

She didn't invite them to sit, so they remained standing.

Katy took the lead. She showed her warrant card. "I'm DI Katy Foster, and these are DI Sally Parker and DS Lorne Warner."

"Am I supposed to be impressed? Why are there three female officers standing in my drawing room?"

"Unfortunately, we have some sad news to share with you."

That piqued Olivia's attention. She sat forward and glared at them. "What news?"

"This afternoon, your son, Nathan, was arrested."

"What? Why? My son has never done anything wrong in his life."

"In your opinion. He was arrested after a shoot-out with an Armed Response Team."

"Impossible. What kind of game are you playing here? I demand to know. No, wait, I think my solicitor should be present before you say anything else." She snatched up her mobile from the coffee table and punched in a single number. "Harry, yes, it's me. I need you up at the house immediately. I have three police officers with me spouting nonsense... Just come, I'll fill you in when you get here." She jabbed a button to end the call and raised her hand. "Don't say another word. He'll be ten minutes. In fact, you can wait in your car. I can't stand the filth being in my house uninvited."

"Very well. It's your choice. We can find our own way out," Katy replied.

Olivia rang a small bell by her side.

The butler appeared within seconds.

"They're leaving. I don't trust them not to snoop around. Will you show them out, Carlton?"

"Yes, m'lady. Come this way," he said, his tone offhand, unlike the last time he'd addressed them.

The butler led them to the front door, and it was slammed shut behind them as they made their way back to the car.

"She must like having egg on her face," Sally muttered before they got in.

Inside the car, Katy and Lorne both sighed.

"I sense she isn't going to take the news well when I deliver it," Katy said.

"Oh well. That's the risk you take when your former husband and offspring are criminals," Lorne said.

They sat there, lost in their own thoughts until a Mercedes came up the drive and drew to a halt in front of them. A man in his late forties flung the driver's door open and flew up the steps. The butler opened the door, and they both looked back to glare at Katy, Sally and Lorne.

After another five-minute wait, the butler came to collect them.

"Here we go for round two," Lorne said. "You don't have to listen to my advice, Katy, but if this were down to me, I'd deliver the news the second we enter the room."

"Yep, already thought about that, Lorne. She's got to learn; she can't mess with the A-Team."

"Be careful," Sally warned. "We've all dealt with her sort before, over the years."

"Haven't we just?" Lorne agreed. "We have strength in numbers and girl power on our side."

They returned to the house. The butler looked each of them up and down in disgust before he allowed them to enter the property.

"This is Harry Davidson, my solicitor," Olivia said.

The man acknowledged them with a brief nod from his position next to the fire.

"Right, now that I have a witness with me, you can tell me why you've come here today."

"Very well," Katy began confidently. "As I stated before, your son, Nathan, was arrested this afternoon." She raised a hand, preventing Olivia and her solicitor from speaking. "Unfortunately, before we had a chance to interview him regarding his involvement in abducting three women—one of them a serving police officer and also his fiancée—he died in his cell."

"What the...?" Olivia screeched and flew out of her chair, her nails ready to claw at Katy's face.

Fortunately, Harry quickly responded and grabbed Olivia's raised hands. "Don't do it, Olivia. We demand to know how this was allowed to happen!" he shouted.

"Although Nathan was searched before being placed in the cell, he had access to a cyanide pill that he must have had hidden. He took the pill and was discovered lying on the floor of his cell."

"You're to blame for this. We'll sue you, the lot of you," Olivia shouted. She shrugged Harry off and returned to the sofa, burying her head in her hands. "Get them the fuck out of my house. Now."

Harry ushered them into the hallway. "I will be making a call to your senior officer. What's his name?"

"DCI Sean Roberts. He accompanied us on the operation today. So, I can assure you, everything was above board when Nathan was arrested."

"Get out. How dare you come here and deliver the news like this to Olivia? You'll be hearing from us in the next few days."

"We look forward to it, sir. Enjoy the rest of your day," Katy said.

They walked back to the car. Katy drove without any of them uttering a word. No one smiled or laughed—that would have been in poor taste.

Once they'd driven out of the gate, Lorne said, "In this job, some days turn out to be far more satisfying than others."

"I agree," Sally and Katy said in unison.

THE END

THANK you for reading The Final Betrayal, the next thrilling adventure is: Garden Of Bones

HAVE you read any of my other fast-paced crime thrillers yet?
Why not try the first book in the DI Sara Ramsey series
No Right To Kill

OR GRAB the first book in the bestselling, award-winning, Justice series here, Cruel Justice

OR THE FIRST book in the spin-off Justice Again series,

Gone in Seconds

Maybe you'd prefer my thriller series set in the stunning Lake District, the first book is To Die For

PERHAPS YOU'D PREFER *to try one of my other police procedural series, the DI Kayli Bright series which begins with*
The Missing Children

OR MAYBE YOU'D *enjoy the DI Sally Parker series set in Norfolk,*
Wrong Place

OR MY GRITTY *police procedural starring DI Nelson set in Manchester, Torn Apart*

OR MAYBE YOU'D *like to try one of my successful psychological thrillers I know The Truth or She's Gone or Shattered Lives*

KEEP IN TOUCH WITH M A COMLEY

Newsletter
http://smarturl.it/8jtcvv

BookBub
www.bookbub.com/authors/m-a-comley

Blog
http://melcomley.blogspot.com

Facebook Readers' Page
https://www.facebook.com/groups/2498593423507951

TikTok
https://www.tiktok.com/@melcomley

ALSO BY M A COMLEY

Blind Justice (Novella)

Cruel Justice (Book #1)

Mortal Justice (Novella)

Impeding Justice (Book #2)

Final Justice (Book #3)

Foul Justice (Book #4)

Guaranteed Justice (Book #5)

Ultimate Justice (Book #6)

Virtual Justice (Book #7)

Hostile Justice (Book #8)

Tortured Justice (Book #9)

Rough Justice (Book #10)

Dubious Justice (Book #11)

Calculated Justice (Book #12)

Twisted Justice (Book #13)

Justice at Christmas (Short Story)

Prime Justice (Book #14)

Heroic Justice (Book #15)

Shameful Justice (Book #16)

Immoral Justice (Book #17)

Toxic Justice (Book #18)

Overdue Justice (Book #19)

Unfair Justice (a 10,000 word short story)

Irrational Justice (a 10,000 word short story)

Seeking Justice (a 15,000 word novella)

Caring For Justice (a 24,000 word novella)

Savage Justice (a 17,000 word novella)

Justice at Christmas #2 (a 15,000 word novella)

Gone in Seconds (Justice Again series #1)

Ultimate Dilemma (Justice Again series #2)

Shot of Silence (Justice Again series #3)

Taste of Fury (Justice Again series #4)

Crying Shame (Justice Again series #5)

See No Evil (Justice Again series #6)

To Die For (DI Sam Cobbs #1)

To Silence Them (DI Sam Cobbs #2)

To Make Them Pay (DI Sam Cobbs #3)

To Prove Fatal (DI Sam Cobbs #4)

To Condemn Them (DI Sam Cobbs #5)

To Punish Them (DI Sam Cobbs #6)

To Entice Them (DI Sam Cobbs #7)

To Control Them (DI Sam Cobbs #8)

To Endanger Lives (DI Sam Cobbs #9)

To Hold Responsible (DI Sam Cobbs #10)

To Catch a Killer (DI Sam Cobbs #11)

To Believe the Truth (DI Sam Cobbs #12)

To Blame Them (DI Sam Cobbs 13)

To Judge Them (DI Sam Cobbs #14)

To Fear Him (DI Sam Cobbs #15)

To Deceive Them (DI Sam Cobbs #16)

To Hurt Them (DI Sam Cobbs #17)

Forever Watching You (DI Miranda Carr thriller)

Wrong Place (DI Sally Parker thriller #1)

No Hiding Place (DI Sally Parker thriller #2)

Cold Case (DI Sally Parker thriller#3)

Deadly Encounter (DI Sally Parker thriller #4)

Lost Innocence (DI Sally Parker thriller #5)

Goodbye My Precious Child (DI Sally Parker #6)

The Missing Wife (DI Sally Parker #7)

Truth or Dare (DI Sally Parker #8)

Where Did She Go? (DI Sally Parker #9)

Sinner (DI Sally Parker #10)

The Good Die Young (DI Sally Parker#11)

Coping Without You (DI Sally Parker #12)

Could It Be Him (DI Sally Parker #13)

Frozen In Time (DI Sally Parker #14)

Echoes of Silence (DI Sally Parker #15)

The Final Betrayal (DI Sally Parker #16)

Garden of Bones (DI Sally Parker #17)

Web of Deceit (DI Sally Parker Novella)

The Missing Children (DI Kayli Bright #1)

Killer On The Run (DI Kayli Bright #2)

Hidden Agenda (DI Kayli Bright #3)

Murderous Betrayal (Kayli Bright #4)

Dying Breath (Kayli Bright #5)

Taken (DI Kayli Bright #6)

The Hostage Takers (DI Kayli Bright Novella)

No Right to Kill (DI Sara Ramsey #1)

Killer Blow (DI Sara Ramsey #2)

The Dead Can't Speak (DI Sara Ramsey #3)

Deluded (DI Sara Ramsey #4)

The Murder Pact (DI Sara Ramsey #5)

Twisted Revenge (DI Sara Ramsey #6)

The Lies She Told (DI Sara Ramsey #7)

For The Love Of... (DI Sara Ramsey #8)

Run for Your Life (DI Sara Ramsey #9)

Cold Mercy (DI Sara Ramsey #10)

Sign of Evil (DI Sara Ramsey #11)

Indefensible (DI Sara Ramsey #12)

Locked Away (DI Sara Ramsey #13)

I Can See You (DI Sara Ramsey #14)

The Kill List (DI Sara Ramsey #15)

Crossing The Line (DI Sara Ramsey #16)

Time to Kill (DI Sara Ramsey #17)

Deadly Passion (DI Sara Ramsey #18)

Son of the Dead (DI Sara Ramsey #19)

Evil Intent (DI Sara Ramsey #20)

The Games People Play (DI Sara Ramsey #21)

Revenge Streak (DI Sara Ramsey #22)

Seeking Retribution (DI Sara Ramsey #23)

Gone... But Where? (DI Sara Ramsey #24)

Last Man Standing (DI Sara Ramsey #25)

Vanished (DI Sara Ramsey #26)

Shadows of Deception (DI Sara Ramsey #27)

I Know The Truth (A Psychological thriller)

She's Gone (A psychological thriller)

Shattered Lives (A psychological thriller)

Evil In Disguise – a novel based on True events

Deadly Act (Hero series novella)

Torn Apart (Hero series #1)

End Result (Hero series #2)

In Plain Sight (Hero Series #3)

Double Jeopardy (Hero Series #4)

Criminal Actions (Hero Series #5)

Regrets Mean Nothing (Hero series #6)

Prowlers (Di Hero Series #7)

Sole Intention (Intention series #1)

Grave Intention (Intention series #2)

Devious Intention (Intention #3)

Cozy mysteries

Murder at the Wedding

Murder at the Hotel

Murder by the Sea

Death on the Coast

Death By Association

Merry Widow (A Lorne Simpkins short story)

It's A Dog's Life (A Lorne Simpkins short story)

A Time To Heal (A Sweet Romance)

A Time For Change (A Sweet Romance)

High Spirits

The Temptation series (Romantic Suspense/New Adult Novellas)

Past Temptation

Lost Temptation

Clever Deception (co-written by Linda S Prather)

Tragic Deception (co-written by Linda S Prather)

Sinful Deception (co-written by Linda S Prather)

Printed in Dunstable, United Kingdom